"Helen, I forbid you to take this job!"

"You can't forbid me to do anything of the kind, Aunt Ada," Helen said. "I'm old enough to make decisions for myself and if people want to talk, then let them. This is a job like any other. I shall be at Brock Castle to teach Lisa Savage, and that's all."

"I hope you know what you're doing," Ada Willis said. Helen silently hoped so, too.

Simon Savage's harsh, shadowy face swam before her eyes. She had found him infinitely disturbing and more than a little frightening.

What if the rumors about him were true?

Scars of Yesterday

by

YVONNE WHITTAL

Harlequin Books

TORONTO • LONDON • NEW YORK • AMSTERDAM
SYDNEY • HAMBURG • PARIS

Original hardcover edition published in 1978
by Mills & Boon Limited

ISBN 0-373-02198-4

Harlequin edition published September 1978

Printed in Canada

CHAPTER ONE

THE lights of Brock Castle filtered strangely through the tall poplars, and Helen Talbot, who had often made use of this private lane as a short cut to her aunt's cottage, brought her Mini to a swift halt, turning off the engine and dousing the headlights almost simultaneously. The eerie darkness settled about her with a silence that made her shiver when a night owl hooted ominously from its perch in the trees.

Brock Castle had stood vacant for almost two years, its high turrets etched sharply against the sky, its vast grounds neglected and overrun with weeds. During the summer holidays, six months ago, she had wandered through its lonely garden contemplating the decision to engage labourers for a cleaning-up expedition, but Aunt Ada had strictly forbidden her interference.

Now, surprisingly, the castle was occupied once again, its lights blinking mockingly at Helen as she sat staring at it with a deep frown marring her smooth brow. It was strange that Aunt Ada had not mentioned it in the letters she had written so frequently, Helen thought, starting the car with an eagerness to substitute the menacing darkness enfolding her for the friendly warmth of her aunt's cottage.

Her foot went down on the accelerator and the Mini shot forward. A frightened hare, caught in the headlights, hesitated momentarily with twitching ears before dashing for cover. The lane dipped sharply and the castle could no longer be seen behind the high stone wall. The solid iron gates, which had rusted on their hinges many years ago, had been repaired and were, for the first time, closed against the friendly inhabitants of Strafford, with a 'Trespassers Will

Be Prosecuted' sign erected as added warning.

A wry smile hovered on Helen's lips as she drove slowly past. The new owner's desire for absolute privacy must have caused plenty of speculation, she decided as she put her foot down once more and sped down the lane. It would be interesting to know more about the new occupants of Brock Castle, and Aunt Ada would no doubt be able to enlighten her, for she owned the only tea-room in the village; a tea-room which Helen had teasingly dubbed the 'News-Room' because of all the scandal passed on from one to the other over a cup of tea and some of Aunt Ada's special cream doughnuts.

'Helen, child, I've been expecting you for the past thirty minutes,' Aunt Ada scolded her some time later after embracing her warmly. 'I've never liked the idea of travelling after dark, and most especially not for a woman on her own.'

'Stop worrying, I've arrived in one piece,' Helen laughed, shedding her coat and placing it on top of her suitcases before following her aunt into the kitchen where a pot of soup stood simmering on the stove.

It was a bright, cosy room, with sunshine yellow curtains drawn across the window. By day one could sit at the scrubbed wooden table and have an excellent view of the cottages further up the hill, as well as the vast red and yellow-wood plantations. But, at seven in the evening, with the curtains drawn against the darkness beyond, it was the straight-backed figure of her aunt that drew her attention.

Ada Willis, matronly in posture and scruplous by nature, had been mother and father to Helen since she was twelve. Losing both her parents in a yachting accident had been a tremendous blow to her, but Aunt Ada, newly widowed herself, had taken Helen under her wing and had made up for the loss in such a wonderful way that Helen considered the years spent with her as the happiest ever.

A plate of hot soup was placed in front of Helen and she smiled her thanks, savouring the tempting aroma before she picked up her spoon.

'Get that into you before we talk,' Aunt Ada said in a tone of voice Helen knew only too well.

As a child, when she had erred, Aunt Ada had used that same tone of voice to indicate her displeasure. Now her displeasure was once again in evidence, and the reason for it was the fact that Helen had resigned her job as a teacher after almost five years' service.

'Why did you do it, Helen?' she demanded the moment Helen pushed her empty plate aside. 'Why throw away years of hard work?'

'This isn't something done on the spur of the moment, Aunt Ada. For some time now I've had the feeling that I was stagnating, so I decided to take a long holiday before I find something more interesting to do.'

'What could be more interesting, or rewarding, than teaching?' Aunt Ada, a teacher herself before marriage, wanted to know. 'And don't smile at me in that tolerant fashion!'

Helen sobered with difficulty and secured a silky strand of fair hair behind her ear. 'Don't you relish the idea of having me at home for a while?'

Her best form of defence against her aunt had always been to attack gently, and she smiled inwardly at her success when Aunt Ada's taut features relaxed.

'It *is* wonderful to have you home again,' she agreed with resignation. 'And, I suppose, at twenty-five you're old enough to know what you are doing.'

The subject was closed, Helen knew, and her aunt would not insist upon an explanation. She observed her aunt thoughtfully while she made the tea, and the years fell away, taking her back to the time she had come to this cottage as a child, and before that. She had been left alone too often in the care of a Coloured servant because of the

wanderlust which had taken her parents to obscure parts of
the world, and, after their death, it had been left to Aunt
Ada to teach her the meaning of discipline. Among other
things, her aunt had taught her to respect the privacy of
another's innermost thoughts and desires. 'Unless they wish
to unburden themselves,' she had told Helen, 'never invade
the privacy of someone else's heart until you are invited to
do so.'

'I saw lights burning in Brock Castle when I passed it,'
Helen remarked as Aunt Ada placed a cup of tea in front of
her on the yellow checkered tablecloth. 'I had no idea it was
no longer unoccupied and I took the usual short cut along
its private lane.'

'Oh, dear,' Aunt Ada shook her grey head sadly.
'Strafford just hasn't been the same since Simon Savage
moved in three months ago with his daughter, and a bevy
of servants.'

'Savage?' Recognition hammered briefly at her brain,
but remained elusive. 'What an extraordinary name! Has
he come here to retire on pension?'

'I shouldn't think so,' Aunt Ada chuckled. 'I caught a
glimpse of him the other day and he certainly appeared too
young for that. I remember being left with the impression
of a dark, ferocious-looking man striding down the street as
if he owned it.'

'His daughter?' Helen prompted, resting her elbows on
the table as she sipped her tea.

'She's seven years old, I believe. Dark and pretty, and
rather pathetic.'

Mischief lurked in the clear blue depths of Helen's eyes
as she met her aunt's steady gaze over the rim of her cup.
'Come on, out with it! What choice bits of scandal have
emanated from that news-room of yours, Aunt Ada?'

'Very little, I'm afraid, except for the snippets of information which have found their way from the Castle
kitchen to the village.' Her aunt's rounded face looked

almost guilty as she continued. 'There was some sort of accident seven months ago, in which his wife and ten-year-old son were killed. More than that I can't tell you, and Mr Savage hasn't exactly charmed the town folk by shutting his gates and erecting that 'Keep Out' sign.'

Helen could well imagine the consternation of the villagers, but she reluctantly had to admit that the new owner had every right to shut them out if he so desired. 'The castle has stood vacant so often that you can't blame anyone for using its grounds as a short cut to the beach, and the previous owners were never fussy in that respect.'

'Well, that's something of the past now,' Aunt Ada said, her hand slicing the air with a gesture of finality. 'Anyone wishing to take a trip to the beach will have to make use of the old path through the lower part of the plantation.'

'Where the ferns and arums have grown out of proportion, and what was left of the path has become slippery with disuse because of the layer of moss,' Helen added thoughtfully.

'Exactly.'

'Couldn't Mr Savage be approached in this respect? Surely, if he was made to understand the circumstances, he might consider re-opening his gates to the public?'

'Simon Savage sees no one, unless he absolutely has to, and then only by appointment,' Aunt Ada sighed heavily. 'No, the danger involved in using the old route is now the responsibility of the Town Council, and I understand that Mr Savage has already instructed them in this respect as he has no intention of allowing his property to become a public thoroughfare.'

'He doesn't sound very pleasant at all.'

'Perhaps you'll realise just how unpleasant when I tell you that he's employed no fewer than four governesses during the past three months, and each one came away swearing never to set foot in Brock Castle again.'

'Governesses?' Helen echoed curiously, giving the discussion her undivided attention for the first time.

'Yes.' The heavy bun at the back of her aunt's head bounced slightly as she nodded. 'His daughter is not well enough to attend a public school, and he's been advertising for someone to give her private tuition and to take charge of the child generally. The last applicant left on Tuesday, and, as far as I know, no one else has applied since.'

Helen's mind went off on a wild excursion as she considered the information her aunt had just divulged. 'I wonder...'

'Helen, you're not thinking of applying, are you?'

She raised her gold-tipped lashes to meet her aunt's direct gaze. 'Why not? I'm at a loose end, looking for a job that's different, and here's one that might prove to be quite a challenge.'

'I understand that he's a cruel, absolutely heartless man,' her aunt tried to dissuade her.

'I'm thinking of his daughter. She obviously needs someone desperately,' Helen argued. 'Do you think, if I wrote to him, he would grant me an interview?'

'I have no doubt that he will, but—'

'Then I'll do so immediately.'

For once, Aunt Ada seemed at a loss for words as she noticed the look of determination on the fine features of the girl opposite her. She possessed an unusual beauty that made most people stop and stare, and her smile, which usually began in the startling blue depths of her eyes before it lifted the corners of her gently curved lips, could be used without difficulty as a weapon against the most hardened heart if she was not so innocently unaware of this. She was not smiling at that moment, however, for the light of battle shone clearly in her eyes. It was a sign that made the older woman sigh with resignation.

'Helen, my dear, think carefully before you involve yourself with this man.'

'There's no harm in applying,' Helen replied airily. 'I

don't have to accept the job if it doesn't appeal to me, but that's a decision I'll have to make after my interview with Mr Savage.'

Helen set off for the Post Office the following morning with her carefully worded letter, requesting an interview, in a sealed envelope in the pocket of her grey slacks. The mild winter sun was warm against her skin as she walked down the street with its thatched cottages nestling against the wooded hillside. She seldom used her car in Strafford, preferring instead to walk through the picturesque little village with its woodland streams, its waterfalls, and its prolific bird life. The Indian Ocean lay invitingly beyond the tall yellow-wood trees, and, during the long cool summers it became a paradise for surfers, beachcombers and fishermen.

She stopped for a moment on a small wooden bridge crossing a fast-running stream that flowed from the hillside, cutting through the grounds of Brock Castle eventually on its eager journey to the ocean. The crystal clear water rippled along stones, rounded and smoothed over the years by the unceasing flow of the stream.

Brock Castle's turrets were clearly visible through the trees, and Helen's thoughts returned swiftly to the reason for her early morning stroll into the village. She was perhaps being hasty in applying for the post of governess at Brock Castle, but it would be something entirely different from the usual routine she had been accustomed to. Exchanging a class of thirty children for one child only could prove to be more strenuous, depending on the child's abilities.

Ever since her fiancé, Richard Laing, had been killed more than a year ago while patrolling the South African border, she had been restless in her job, and desired a change that would make her forget, to some extent, the cavity his death had left. Her eventual resignation had come as no surprise to her colleagues, but, after spending the first two weeks of her holiday in the lush wine-growing valleys of the Cape, she was more than ready to abandon her plans for a lengthy trip across the country in favour of the post advertised at Brock Castle.

Simon Savage. Why did she have this persistent feeling that she ought to know the name?

The peace and tranquillity of her surroundings was disturbed by the sound of children's laughter as they played hide and seek among the trees, and, smiling slightly at their display of exuberance, she stepped off the bridge and made her way to the small stone building some distance away.

'I hope you're not applying for that job advertised at the castle,' Edwina Adams, the postmistress, remarked in astonishment, staring at Helen over the rim of her spectacles after glancing at the address on the envelope.

'Why not?' Helen laughed, shaking off the slight feeling of uneasiness. 'Is there any reason why I shouldn't apply?'

'I can think of almost half a dozen reasons, and four of them left Strafford after just a few weeks at Brock Castle.'

Helen's smile flashed confidently. 'In that case, let's hope I manage to remain a little longer.'

'I hope you know what you're doing, Helen,' Edwina replied in a tight-lipped fashion as she stamped the envelope. 'Mr Savage has his post collected at eleven each morning, so I'll just drop this into his box.'

'Thank you, Mrs Adams.'

As she stepped out into the sunlight once more, Helen drew the tangy air deep into her lungs before making her way towards Aunt Ada's tea-room, where the smell of freshly baked scones met her at the entrance.

A stockily built young man in grey flannels and tweed jacket stood chatting to her aunt at the counter, but they ceased their conversation the moment Helen joined them.

'Helen, I would like you to meet Dr Toby Warren. He's taken over from old Dr Murray,' Aunt Ada introduced her brightly.

The unruly brown head turned and a cool grey glance appraised Helen with obvious pleasure. His glance shifted from her shoulder-length silvery fair hair, down the length of her slender, but shapely figure in candy-striped blouse and grey slacks. Those cool eyes met hers once more, and his strong features relaxed into a smile.

'I've heard so much about you, Miss Talbot, but no one took the trouble to tell me that you were beautiful as well.'

His voice had a warm, friendly quality to it that was pleasing to the ear, while his handclasp was firm ... and lingering. Helen coloured slightly and laughed away her embarrassment.

'Are you always this outspoken, Dr Warren?'

'I don't believe in hiding my feelings,' he admitted, releasing her hand at last with obvious reluctance. 'I do enough of that in my profession, but in private I speak my mind.'

'An admirable quality, but not always a wise one,' Helen remarked, aware of her aunt's encouraging glance.

'Perhaps,' Toby Warren agreed, glancing regretfully at his wrist watch. 'Miss Talbot, I have a few calls to make, but may I pay you a visit this evening at your home?'

Out of the corner of her eye she could see Aunt Ada's smile broadening with pleasure, and her own lips curved into a smile as she said politely, 'I shall look forward to seeing you again, Dr Warren.'

He nodded briefly and excused himself, striding from the tea-room and out across the street to where his car was parked.

'Toby Warren is such a nice young man.'

'Aunt Ada,' Helen warned, turning to face the older woman across the counter. 'Don't start your matchmaking on my first day home! Besides, I have no intention of becoming emotionally involved with a man just yet.'

'It's time you forgot about Richard, my dear, and locked him away in the past where he belongs,' her aunt said tritely, glancing about the empty tea-room to make sure that there was no one to eavesdrop on their conversation. 'Every woman needs to love and be loved, Helen, and most especially you. You have a warm and generous nature that should be directed at a husband and children of your own, and the longer you wait, the more fastidious you'll become, until you eventually find yourself on the shelf.'

Helen moved her shoulders uncomfortably. 'I have no desire to become an old maid, Aunt Ada, but—'

'Then I suggest you do something about it quickly,' her aunt interrupted persuasively. 'You're twenty-five; an age when most women are married already with a family of their own. You can't afford to wait much longer.'

If anyone other than Aunt Ada had spoken to her in this manner, Helen might have lost her temper—something she seldom did—but instead she laughed merrily, the sound echoing through the cosy intimacy of the tea-room. 'Good heavens, Aunt Ada! You surely don't expect me to marry the first man who comes along?'

Aunt Ada shook her head firmly. 'No, child, but don't reject every man on sight. Give yourself the opportunity to get to know them better.'

Blue eyes sparkled with humour. 'Meaning Toby Warren?'

'A man in his profession needs a wife,' Aunt Ada muttered with a guilty expression on her slightly flushed face.

Helen shook her head with mock disapproval. 'I can see you've made up your mind about whom he should marry!'

'Don't deprive an old woman of her dreams, child.'

Her grey eyes grew misty, and Helen leaned impulsively across the counter to plant a kiss on her soft cheek. 'Dreams don't always come true, Aunt Ada, but I promise to be nice to Toby Warren whenever we meet, if that will make you happy.'

Helen dressed with care that evening for Toby Warren's

promised visit. With her pale blue woollen dress cut in the latest loose-fitting fashion, and her hair brushed to a silvery sheen, she looked wholesome and fresh with the barest touch of make-up on her face. She had been blessed with a clear skin that warranted little attention, except in the summer months when the sun played havoc with her fairness.

With a final critical glance at herself in the mirror, she closed her bedroom door behind her and went through to the lounge where Aunt Ada sat knitting in front of the log fire. She beamed her approval as Helen joined her, and lowered her knitting for a moment.

'You're the image of your mother, my dear, and I thought her the most beautiful woman I'd ever seen when your father brought her home for the first time to meet our parents.'

Aunt Ada's glance became reminiscent, and Helen swallowed at the inevitable lump that always rose in her throat whenever they discussed her parents. 'They *were* happy together, weren't they, Aunt Ada?'

'Yes, child,' she nodded reassuringly before picking up her knitting once more, 'and you made their happiness complete, although they were forced to leave you behind eventually when their travels interfered with your education.'

The log fire crackled and sent a shower of sparks up the chimney. When Helen was a child, the winter evenings spent by the fireside had been the most enjoyable, with Aunt Ada dipping into her vast supply of stories with which to amuse her.

Toby Warren's knock on the front door interrupted Helen's brief nostalgia, and she rose swiftly to admit him. He made no effort to hide his admiration and, although she was accustomed to the admiring glances of strange men, she flushed deeply as she extricated her hand from his and preceded him into the lounge.

'Toby, dear boy,' Aunt Ada welcomed him, drawing a chair closer to hers. 'Come and sit down here beside me so I can measure the length of your arm.'

'It's extremely kind of you, Mrs Willis, to knit this sweater for me,' he said warmly as they joined her in front of the fire. 'I understand that the winter evenings can be quite chilly here in Strafford, but so far the weather has been surprisingly mild.'

Their voices droned on, but Helen no longer heard what they were saying as, for the first time, she paid particular attention to the garment Aunt Ada was knitting. So, she thought as she smiled inwardly, her aunt had collected another waif for whom to care. Her habit of temporarily adopting people, young or old, was something Helen had grown accustomed to over the years, and it was only logical that Dr Toby Warren, alone and without a wife, should be the latest recipient of her motherly care and concern. He had that 'little boy lost' look about him, she noticed as she sat back and watched Aunt Ada taking his measurements, and it was a look that never failed to stir her aunt's heart-strings.

She glanced up suddenly to find him staring at her, and he grinned sheepishly. 'Your aunt has been spoiling me ever since I arrived in this village four months ago.'

'Aunt Ada is a great spoiler,' Helen admitted, her teasing glance directed at her aunt. 'She can also be terribly bossy at times when she thinks it her duty to manipulate the people she cares about.'

'Nonsense,' Aunt Ada muttered, unabashed. 'I don't spoil people, and neither am I bossy, but when someone buries their head stubbornly in the sand like an ostrich, there's only one thing to do, and that's to pull it out.'

'It's amazing how often people are inclined to behave in that fashion,' Toby remarked innocently.

'Yes ... amazing,' Aunt Ada agreed, glancing significantly at Helen before she picked up her knitting once more, the needles tapping out a message that ignited a spark of humour in Helen.

'Have I said something I shouldn't have?' Toby asked as Helen laughed outright.

'No,' she giggled, wondering what he would say if he should discover that he was unwittingly involved in her aunt's subtle accusation. 'Aunt Ada was merely taking a private dig at me, and she scored a definite point.'

Toby Warren did not pretend that he understood the reason for her amusement, and neither did he press for an explanation, which was something to be thankful for.

As the evening progressed she began to relax in his company as they shed the cloak of formality with ease, and drifted into the use of first names. She liked his sincere approach to life, and his down-to-earth assessment of people's problems. Toby Warren, she decided as she went through to the kitchen to make tea, was an extremely likeable man, and the first, since Richard's death, to capture her interest.

'Your aunt told me this morning that you were thinking of applying for that job at Brock Castle,' Toby remarked after Aunt Ada had tactfully retired.

'I'm not just thinking about it, I've already applied.'

Toby flicked his cigarette into the fire and leaned forward in his chair with his elbows on his knees. 'I don't wish to interfere, Helen, but do you think it was wise of you to do so?'

Helen lowered her head, allowing her hair to fall forward and cast a shadow across her face to hide her expression. 'Tell me, Toby, why is everyone so determined to advise me against it?'

'Everyone?'

'Well ... first it was Aunt Ada, then Edwina Adams at the Post Office, and now you.'

Toby shifted uncomfortably and stared hard at the dying

embers of the log fire. 'I'm not advising you against it, but I wonder whether you've realised that, if you get the job, it would mean living in at Brock Castle.'

'What's so terrible about that?'

He coloured slightly, but his grey glance met hers steadily. 'You'll be living alone and unchaperoned with Simon Savage and his daughter, Lisa.'

Lisa. So that was the name of Mr Savage's daughter, she thought as she laughed briefly at Toby's discomfort.

'I'm not the kind of woman who mixes business with pleasure, Toby, and neither, I'm sure, is Mr Savage looking for an affair so soon after his wife's death.'

'You're a very beautiful woman, Helen,' he stated calmly. 'Beautiful enough to change the mind of a hardened bachelor.'

His statement held a certain significance she could not help noticing. Was he referring to himself? she wondered, her heartbeat quickening uncomfortably.

'Have you met Mr Savage?' she asked, changing the subject swiftly before the conversation became too personal.

'Very briefly when I was called in to take a look at his daughter one evening,' he admitted, settling back in his chair.

'What's he like?'

There was a certain urgency in her request which she could not define even to herself; an inexplicable interest in the man she hoped to work for, a man whose name alone had the power to disturb her calmly disciplined nerves.

'I think I shall leave you to find out for yourself,' Toby laughed teasingly. 'We could always compare notes afterwards.'

Helen frowned slightly. 'I wonder whether he'll think my application worth considering.'

'From what I can gather, he must be getting pretty desperate in his efforts to stabilise his daughter's studies, but he won't have much success unless he changes his attitude towards the child.'

'His attitude?' she echoed curiously.

'Lisa Savage isn't allowed much freedom to indulge in childish games. She's become a repressed, sullen little girl, and it's Simon Savage's instructions as to her upbringing which has been the true bone of contention between him and the previous governesses,' Toby enlightened her, gesturing distastefully with his hands. 'Look, let's talk about ourselves for a moment and forget the problems at Brock Castle. There's a delightful little restaurant in Mossel Bay that serves the best crayfish in the district. How about having dinner there with me one evening next week?'

He captured her hands, the pressure of his fingers gently persuasive as she stared at him thoughtfully, unable as yet to tear her thoughts from the subject they had been discussing.

'Helen?' Toby prompted, his grey eyes searching hers until he had her undivided attention.

'I would like very much to have dinner with you, Toby.'

Later, when she accompanied him out to the gate, her glance turned irresistibly in the direction of Brock Castle. What *really* went on behind those stone walls? she wondered curiously. Were father and daughter still suffering from the aftermath of the accident which had disrupted their lives, or was there a more sinister explanation for their behaviour?

The people in the village were strangely reticent about the subject, but when the name Savage was mentioned, their expressions sobered instantly.

'When do I see you again?' Toby interrupted her thoughts.

'Oh, I ... don't know,' she replied vaguely. 'You did ask me to have dinner with you one evening.'

'But that's a week away,' he protested. his pained expression clearly visible as the moon slid from behind a cloud.

'Strafford is a small village, Toby,' she reminded him humorously. 'We're bound to see quite a lot of each other.'

If there was one thing Dr Toby Warren was made to realise with clarifying swiftness, then it was the fact that this silvery girl, who blended so exquisitely with the moonlight, had no intention of allowing herself to be rushed into a lasting relationship.

'I'll see you around, as they say,' he told her calmly. 'Goodnight, Helen.'

The rear lights of his car disappeared down the hill, and Helen sighed inwardly. Toby could prove to be a valued friend, but she hoped fervently that he had no intention of demanding more than friendship from her in the future. Despite Aunt Ada's claim that it was time she settled down, she could not somehow visualise herself as a doctor's wife. Besides, it would take someone special to re-awaken her heart after the love she had known with Richard Laing.

She shivered suddenly as the cool breeze coiled about her, and she hurried inside to seek the dying warmth of the log fire in the lounge. The conversation she had had with Toby, concerning Simon Savage, was churning through her mind at a confusing pace. With everyone's warnings echoing in her ears, it was difficult to judge the wisdom of her decision to approach Mr Savage for employment. It had seemed so temptingly different initially, but doubts were now beginning to mar her excitement.

It was too late to recall her letter of application, so there was nothing else she could do but push through to the interview. No one could force her to take the position he offered, she told herself reassuringly, and she would be quite at liberty to turn it down if it did not appeal to her.

This thought offered a meagre comfort to her as she switched off the lights and went to her room, but it was of Brock Castle that she dreamed that night, its occupants taking the shape of dark, shadowy figures that remained faceless as she struggled back from the encasing depths of oblivion. For endless minutes she lay staring into the darkness, centring her thoughts on more pleasant things, until she eventually drifted into a dreamless sleep.

CHAPTER TWO

THE summons to call at Brock Castle was delivered by hand shortly after lunch the following day, and Helen read through the short note a second time as if to convince herself of its cryptic contents.

'Dear Miss Talbot,' it began in a firm, legible handwriting, 'I shall expect you at seven this evening. Please bring the necessary references with respect to the position in question.' It was signed, 'S. Savage.'

There was no question of whether the mentioned hour would be convenient for her, merely a command she was expected to obey. With half a mind to telephone Brock Castle for the purpose of telling Simon Savage exactly what he could do with his job, Helen marched into the hallway and lifted the receiver. Then her sense of humour came to the rescue, and she abandoned the idea in favour of keeping the stipulated appointment, regardless of the unfavourable impression she had gained.

To meet this man, who displayed such arrogance in so few words, had now become a must. If the encounter did not turn out to be a fruitful one, it would at least have been interesting, she told herself with conviction.

Aunt Ada was not too impressed when she arrived home late that afternoon and discovered that the reason for Helen's activity in the kitchen was due to the fact that she had an early appointment with Simon Savage.

'One would think he would have the decency to arrange an interview at a more respectable hour during the day,' her aunt fumed, discarding her coat and tying an apron about her waist.

'Let's not condemn him outright,' Helen sprang inexplicably to his defence. 'Mr Savage may have a plausible reason for wishing to conduct the interview at this hour.'

Aunt Ada muttered something unintelligible, but did not pursue the subject, maintaining a stony silence until they sat down to dinner. 'Why don't you give Toby a ring and ask him to accompany you?'

'And give Mr Savage the impression that I was afraid to cross his threshold alone? No, thank you,' Helen shook her head firmly. 'I shall meet him alone, or not at all.'

Her fearless statement recoiled on her, however, as she drove up to Brock Castle later that evening. She wished at that moment that she had not been so hasty in rejecting Aunt Ada's suggestion to invite Toby Warren along. He was just as much a stranger to her, yet she knew that she would have felt safe with him.

'Safe?' her thoughts echoed mockingly. 'Safe from what?'

The lights of her Mini sliced through the shadowy darkness and flashed across the brass plaque with the name 'Brock Castle' engraved on it, and then the enormous iron gates were ahead of her.

'What now?' she asked herself aloud as she tapped the brake and reduced speed. 'Do I get out and drag them open, or am I supposed to lean on the hooter until someone comes along?'

Still pondering her dilemma, she brought the Mini to a dead stop less than a metre away from the gates, but the next moment her lips parted in an audible gasp. She stared in hypnotic fascination as those heavy gates swung open on oiled hinges to admit her, like the jaws of some gigantic animal waiting to devour its unsuspecting prey.

Simon Savage had obviously had a mechanical device installed to operate those cumbersome gates, she thought, shivering slightly as they closed behind her. She experienced a weird feeling that she had been trapped, but, shaking off her sombre thoughts, she followed the curved road through the tall poplar trees up to the Castle which had been built so many years ago to the specification of a retired couple from England.

Helen's legs were shaking when she eventually climbed the stone steps on to the wide terrace. The light was on in the living-room, but the curtains had been drawn, allowing only a strip of light to show. It was an exceptionally dark night, for the clouds had gathered earlier that afternoon with the promise of rain. She had never been afraid of the darkness, but the eerie silence surrounding her at that moment made her shiver as though a cold hand had slid down the length of her spine. Admonishing herself with a silent rebuke, she raised the heavy brass knocker and knocked twice.

The door opened almost instantly and a man in uniform admitted her, his brown face expressionless as he enquired her name, and led the way through the large, dimly lit hall. It was two years since she had last had the pleasure of visiting Brock Castle, she thought as she caught a glimpse of the shadowy steps with the ornately carved balustrade leading to the upper floor, but there was no time to take in her surroundings as she followed the stiff-backed servant into the well-lit living-room.

'The master is in the study,' he said, gesturing to the door at the other end of the room. 'The madam can go in.'

Helen smiled her thanks with a nervous flutter at the pit of her stomach, and the man bowed slightly before leaving, his footsteps silent on the carpeted floor. She glanced about her swiftly, but was aware of nothing except the closed door, beyond which Simon Savage was waiting to interview her. She swallowed nervously and her hand rose unnecessarily to her hair before she approached the door and knocked.

'Come in,' a deep voice commanded, and Helen turned

the polished brass handle and stepped inside on rubbery legs. A small desk lamp threw a clear light across the papers on the large ebony desk, but other than that there was only the glow of the log fire to further illuminate the room. 'My God, it's Helen in person!'

Coming from the brightly lit living-room, she was momentarily blinded, as well as confused by his remark. 'I—I beg your pardon?'

'The Trojan lady whose face, supposedly, launched a thousand ships,' the deep voice explained, its owner taking frightening shape before her as she searched vainly for a suitable reply. Tall, dark and broad-shouldered, he somehow managed to keep his face in the shadows as he took her coat from her. 'Sit down, Miss Talbot.'

Helen did as she was told, but the man before her remained standing with his back to the light. He had the unfair advantage of being able to see her quite clearly, while she was allowed nothing more than the outline of a proudly held head and a lean, muscular body. His features remained concealed from her, but she was aware of the deliberate inspection his eyes were making. Her skin felt warm, but she hoped that the faint colouring of her cheeks went unnoticed.

'Where are you from?'

Startled by the sound of his voice, her nerves jumped violently, but she managed to reply with a calmness that gave no hint of the butterflies let loose inside of her. 'I've been teaching in Cape Town for the past five years, but Strafford has been my home since I was twelve.'

'What made you apply for this position?'

'I need a job, Mr Savage, and you're offering one.'

The proud head tilted slightly. 'I never advertised it in the local paper recently.'

'No,' she admitted, clutching at her handbag. 'My aunt told me that you—you might need someone.'

'Your aunt?' he queried with slight incredulity.

'Ada Willis,' she explained quickly. 'She owns the tea-room in the village.'

'Hm...' The logs crackled loudly during the ensuing silence, and Helen wondered foolishly whether being Ada Willis' niece would spoil her chances. 'You have brought references?'

'Yes, I——' She faltered as she handed him the sheaf of papers and raised her glance. He had stepped forward into the column of light, and she found herself staring at the disfiguring scar running from temple to jaw on the right side of his face. Her stomach nerves tightened with a sickening jolt, but the challenge in his dark eyes brought her to her senses. 'I think you will find my references in order.'

His eyes flamed with mockery, but she held his glance steadily, and remained silent. After the initial shock, his scar went unnoticed as she felt the staggering power of his glance pinning her to her chair and reducing her to a trembling mass of awareness. Did he have this effect on everyone, she wondered agitatedly as he finally lowered his glance to examine the papers she had handed to him, or was it merely the imaginative eeriness of her surroundings that made her feel this way?

The hand that flicked over the pages was well-shaped, with strong fingers and short, well-kept nails, she noticed absently, raising her glance surreptitiously to observe him. His hair was dark, almost black in the dim light, the forehead broad, with thick black eyebrows coming together in a frown that looked anything but promising. The bridge of his nose was high and straight, the mouth firm, with a tendency to appear cynical, and the skin was drawn tightly over shallow cheekbones down to a square chin. It was a harsh face, she decided tentatively, allowing for the unkind light which accentuated the hollows and planes of his features.

'You have no experience in private tutoring, I notice,' he

said eventually, returning her references and lowering himself on to the edge of his desk.

'No, I haven't,' she admitted, instantly on the defensive. 'But whether you teach one or thirty, it's basically the same.'

'Not entirely, Miss Talbot,' he contradicted coldly. 'The job I am offering is that of governess, which means that you will be in demand day and night. Do you think you could cope with such a situation?'

'I don't see why not. I'm very fond of children.'

His eyes flicked over her with mocking intensity. 'You're very young, Miss Talbot.'

Her chin rose defiantly. 'I'm twenty-five.'

'You're very young,' he repeated, as if she had not spoken. 'Too young for the position I'm offering.'

Helen experienced a sinking feeling that was totally inexplicable. 'Are you turning down my application, Mr Savage?'

The silence was unnerving as they faced each other, her question hanging heavily in the air between them. She suspected the reason for his indecision and wondered at the outcome.

'I can't afford to turn down your application, just like that,' he snapped his fingers, making her jump. 'But I must confess that an older woman would have been more suitable. I live alone with my daughter, Miss Talbot, and, if I should employ you, it would mean that you would have to make your home with us. An older woman's presence in my home would not be questioned, but someone as young as yourself would arouse unsavoury speculation.'

Helen coloured slightly. 'I realise that, Mr Savage.'

'The realisation does not appear to trouble you much,' he observed dryly with a flicker of cynical amusement in his watchful eyes.

'No, it doesn't,' she confirmed coolly, sustaining his

glance and hoping that her heightened colour would go unnoticed yet again.

'Why did you resign your previous post?' he asked at length.

'I needed a change, and I wanted to get away from Cape Town.'

'Was there a man involved in this decision?'

'Indirectly, yes.' She clutched at the arms of her chair to steady her trembling hands, and decided that a simple acceptance or rejection would be preferable to this prolonged interview. 'Mr Savage, I——'

'Did your aunt suggest that you should approach me?' he interrupted with an abruptness that shattered her nerve.

'No, she advised against it.'

The corners of his mouth twitched slightly, but that was all. 'Your honesty is commendable.'

'Do I get the job?' she asked, ignoring the disturbing mockery of his searching gaze.

'Miss Talbot, my daughter has lost a tremendous amount with regard to her education during the past months, and, circumstances being as they are, I should turn you away at once, but I can't afford to allow the situation to linger on indefinitely.'

'Does this mean——?'

'It means that the job is yours, if you still want to accept it after I've given you all the details.'

'Thank you,' she sighed, relaxing in her chair with a feeling of satisfaction she could not entirely explain.

'Don't thank me yet, Miss Talbot,' he mocked, rising to his feet and moving beyond the column of light to become a shadowy figure once more. 'Lisa is a highly strung, oversensitive child. Ever since we were involved in the accident which killed my wife and son, Lisa has been suffering from depressing nightmares at night. She has become subdued and sullen, and needs plenty of attention—something which I can't give her at the moment. Because of this nervous disorder the doctors advised that she be taught at home until such time as she's able to attend school in the normal way. I'm hoping this will be at the end of the year, but that depends entirely on Lisa's progress.'

'How old is she, Mr Savage?'

'She'll be eight in January next year,' he said abruptly, resuming his seat on the edge of the desk with a look on his face that stilled the numerous questions hovering on her lips. 'I hope that the salary I'm offering is satisfactory to you,' he continued, mentioning an amount that made her head spin. 'If you're willing to risk the consequences involved, as well as taking on a problematic child, how soon may I expect you to take up residence here at Brock Castle?'

She licked her lips nervously. 'Whenever it would suit you.'

'Tomorrow after lunch?'

'Yes,' she whispered, slightly breathless at the speed with which things were happening.

'Good,' he said, rising to his feet to signify that the interview was at an end. 'It will give you the week-end to become acquainted with Lisa before you start lessons on Monday.'

He held her coat for her, and Helen slipped into it, in a hurry now to get away from this disturbing man who was giving her the ever-increasing feeling that he could be as savage as the name he carried.

He was not unaware of her nervous haste, she realised, for he raised his eyebrows in a mocking gesture. 'You know the way out?'

'Yes,' she whispered huskily. 'Goodnight, Mr Savage.'

At the door she glanced back briefly, but he had turned away, her presence no longer of any importance to him. She paused for a moment in the living-room, taking in the heavily padded armchairs and sombre curtains. The furnishings were unimaginative and depressing, as if someone had, with deliberate intent, created an atmosphere that lacked warmth and gaiety. Compared to the warmth of the dimly lit study she had just left, this room was cold and cheerless, Helen thought, shivering slightly as she made her way into the hall.

A flash of white caught her eyes on the landing above, but the next moment it was gone. His daughter perhaps? she wondered, straining her eyes as she stared up into the darkness. After four governesses coming and going over the past weeks, could one blame her for her curiosity as to the appearance of the next?

'Have you lost your way?' a mocking voice inquired behind her, and Helen swung round sharply to stare up into the scarred face of Simon Savage.

'N-no,' she stammered as her heart leapt into her throat to create a paralysing effect on her vocal cords which, fortunately, did not last long. 'I thought I caught a glimpse of someone on the landing.'

Heavy eyebrows ascended with distinct mockery. 'This castle isn't haunted as far as I know.'

'Not to my knowledge either,' she remarked stiffly, pulling herself together with an effort. 'It could have been one of your servants, I suppose.'

'Most probably,' he conceded with a slightly bored expression as he stepped past her to open the front door. 'Goodnight again, Miss Talbot.'

This time Helen did not hesitate, and, clutching her handbag and the envelope containing her papers, she mumbled something and hurried outside. A gentle rain was falling, the fine spray cool against her flaming cheeks as she climbed into her car. She did not dare look back to see if he was still standing in the open doorway, but every nerve seemed to tell her that his dark eyes had followed the lights of her Mini down the drive as if to make sure that she left the premises. The gates opened noiselessly at her approach, and an inaudible sigh of relief escaped her as she passed through them and turned left down the lane, leaving Brock Castle and the inscrutable Simon Savage behind her.

'Well?' Aunt Ada demanded when Helen arrived back at the cottage some minutes later.

'You see before you the new governess at Brock Castle,' Helen announced, curtsying dramatically.

'Don't be flippant, girl,' her aunt rebuked her agitatedly, drawing a chair closer to the fire. 'Sit down and tell me what happened.'

'Nothing spectacular happened,' Helen told her as she sat down and leaned closer to the fire to warm her hands, but that was not strictly the truth. One could not meet a man like Simon Savage and come away unaffected by his overpowering personality. 'Mr Savage would have preferred an older woman because the job requires that she should live in, but...' She shrugged lightly as she stared into the flames, 'I don't think he can afford to be choosy at the moment.'

'Helen,' Aunt Ada began, her knitting lying forgotten in her laps as she focused a disapproving glance on her niece, 'please tell me you haven't accepted the position?'

'I have, Aunt Ada,' she replied quietly, the fire warming her cold cheeks. 'I'm expected at Brock Castle after lunch tomorrow.'

Her aunt stared at her with something akin to horror, a tell-tale nerve jumping at the side of her mouth as a sign that she was deeply disturbed. 'Have you considered the consequences?'

'Yes, Aunt Ada,' Helen nodded, her voice gently teasing to lighten the tension. 'Mr Savage, his daughter and I will be alone at night when his servants retire to their quarters, and the wagging tongues of the villagers will whisper and speculate about what goes on after dark between Strafford's newest inhabitant and his female employee.' She laughed shortly with a touch of unaccustomed cynicism. 'I can just imagine their queries. "Are they having a passionate affair in the shrubbery, or has he slapped her into chains and seduced her in the cellar?" '

'It's nothing to joke about,' Aunt Ada rebuked her sharply, her matronly figure bristling with agitation.

'I'm not joking,' Helen assured her aunt seriously. 'People can be vicious when they choose to be.'

They faced each other in absolute silence and, as on so many occasions in the past, their wills clashed. The older woman's hands clutched the arms of her chair, her expression stern and disapproving.

'Helen, I forbid you to take this job.'

Her tone of voice said more than her actual words, but on this occasion Helen refused to be intimidated. 'You can't forbid me to do anything of the kind, Aunt Ada. I'm old enough to make decisions for myself, and if people want to talk, then let them. As far as I'm concerned, this is a job just like any other, and my conscience is clear on that subject. I shall be at Brock Castle to teach Lisa Savage, and that's all.'

Despite her efforts Ada Willis could not hide the glimmer of admiration in her eyes as she said primly, 'I hope you know what you're doing.'

'So do I,' Helen admitted with a hint of amusement in her solemn expression.

'I can't pretend I'm happy about it, but I shall stand by you no matter what happens. I trust your integrity, but I don't trust that ferocious-looking young man.'

'For goodness' sake, Aunt Ada, what could he possibly do to me?' Helen protested laughingly. 'The man isn't some kind of a monster!'

Aunt Ada frowned and resumed her knitting with a certain vengefulness. 'I never said he was a monster, but he is a man, and all men are basically the same. When they see a pretty face...'

She left her sentence unfinished, but the unspoken insinuation lingered between them uncomfortably. Her aunt's statement had, however, swivelled Helen's thoughts in a different direction from the one intended.

'You never told me his face was badly scarred,' Helen remarked casually as she kicked off her shoes and wriggled her toes while she held them towards the fire.

'I had no idea that it was,' Aunt Ada replied swiftly. 'I caught a very brief glimpse of him one day, but not enough to notice his features.'

Simon Savage's harsh, shadowy face swam before Helen's eyes, and she blinked rapidly to disperse with his image. She had found him infinitely disturbing, and more than a little frightening, but it was difficult to judge his character after their brief encounter that evening.

'I wonder what the child is like,' she spoke her thoughts out loud.

'You'll know tomorrow.'

'Yes . . .'

The wisdom of her decision was debatable, but it was the challenge she had been seeking; that 'something different' from the usual teaching post she had wanted to escape from. Mr Savage had given her a brief insight into his daughter's problems, but Helen realised that she would have to play it entirely by ear, a thought that filled her with a measure of anxiety when she lingered on the possibility that she might be unsuccessful in gaining the child's confidence.

The telephone interrupted her thoughts, and she rose to answer it while Aunt Ada went through to the kitchen to make a pot of tea. To Helen's surprise it was Toby Warren, and she warmed instantly to the sound of his voice.

'I don't have to take surgery tomorrow afternoon,' he began coaxingly. 'What about taking a drive into the country with me?'

Helen bit her lip with disappointment, and said apologetically, 'I'm sorry, Toby, but I shan't be able to. I have to report for duty at Brock Castle tomorrow afternoon.'

'You don't mean to tell me he actually gave you the job?' he asked in disbelief.

'Yes, he did.'

'I wonder if you realise what you're letting yourself in for.'

She was becoming a little tired of these cynical observations, she thought, her fingers tightening on the receiver. 'I know exactly what I'm doing, Toby.'

'I've just been at Brock Castle to see Lisa Savage,' he informed her, and she held her breath slightly as she waited for him to continue. 'She was in a highly nervous state when I arrived, and I was forced to administer a light sedative. These recurring nightmares she suffers from are wearing the child out completely.'

'Do you think that I may have something to do with her illness this evening?' she asked with concern. 'Mr Savage must surely have told her he was expecting me tomorrow. Do you think the thought of a new governess, a complete stranger, might have brought on this attack of nerves?'

'It's possible.'

'Oh, dear!' Helen sighed miserably.

'You're going to come up against quite a few problems, Helen, but if you ever need help and advice, you know I shall be only too happy to oblige.'

To have Dr Toby Warren to turn to for advice gave her a certain amount of confidence. 'That's very kind of you, Toby. Thank you.'

'Don't thank me,' he laughed briefly. 'Let me know when you have a free afternoon, or evening, and I'll arrange my schedule accordingly. We still have a dinner date, remember?'

'I know,' she smiled to herself. 'We may have to postpone it a little, but I'll contact you just as soon as I've settled down into a regular routine.'

Helen's mood was thoughtful when she resumed her seat

beside the fire. Her confidence was ebbing swiftly, to leave her with the disturbing thought that she had foolishly ventured into something of which she had no knowledge, or experience.

Aunt Ada's glance was curious as she brought in the tray of tea and placed it on the low stinkwood table between them, but Helen kept her face averted, refusing to meet those searching eyes that seldom missed anything.

They drank their tea in silence, the clock on the wall ticking away the minutes in a relentless fashion, and bringing with it a new and unaccustomed tension that stilted the relaxed atmosphere which had always prevailed between her aunt and herself.

'It's not too late to change your mind.'

Helen's silvery fair head rose sharply, a smile flickering across her face at the shrewdness of her aunt's guess. 'What would Mr Savage think of me if I backed out now?'

'Does it matter what he thinks of you?'

Yes, it did matter, she thought, a little tremor quivering along her nerves to settle hollowly at the pit of her stomach. She could imagine the mockery in his dark eyes, and the cynical twist of those firm lips should she confront him with the statement that she had changed her mind. It was a woman's prerogative, so they said, yet she knew instinctively that Simon Savage would consider it an act of cowardice.

'Would I be able to live with myself in future, knowing that I'd been too afraid to accept the challenge Mr Savage had offered?' Helen shook her head slowly, and supplied the answer to her own question. 'I don't think so. I would want to hide from myself at the thought that I'd surrendered to my fears without even trying.'

Ada Willis sighed and resigned herself to the situation as she helped herself to more tea. 'You never could resist a challenge, and in that respect you're so very much like your father used to be. My greatest fear was that you would inherit his wanderlust, and for the past five years I'd been almost certain that you hadn't, but now I'm not so sure.'

'I *have* been considering a working holiday through the country,' Helen admitted thoughtfully. 'There's so much of South Africa that I haven't seen yet.'

'Nonsense,' Aunt Ada snorted, brushing aside the idea. 'It isn't right for a women to go traipsing all over the country on her own. What you need is to settle down with a husband and to start raising a family.'

Helen smiled and stared dreamily into the fire. 'Marriage isn't for me, Aunt Ada ... not just yet anyway. I've grown accustomed to my freedom, and I would like to keep it that way for a little longer.'

Her aunt seemed about to argue, but changed her mind and lapsed into a silence that was somehow less strained.

When they eventually turned out the lights and went to bed, Helen felt nothing more than a touch of apprehension for the future. Lisa Savage would soon discover that she had no need to fear her new governess, but, for some strange reason, Helen had the feeling that Simon Savage would be far less co-operative than his daughter. He possessed a core of steel which she had been acutely conscious of while in his presence; a cynical harshness which had made it difficult for her to imagine him the father of a young and sensitive child.

Her thoughts turned again to the conversation she had had with Toby, and this time she was convinced that Mr Savage was just as much to blame for his daughter's illness. It largely depended on how much tact he had employed when telling his daughter about her new governess, and, somehow, she could not attribute that quality to a man like Simon Savage.

His dark face was before her, the scar on his cheek slightly raised and livid, while his eyes accused her harshly. Guilt made her force his image from her mind as she brushed her hair with added vigour. She was basing her deductions on supposition, and it was unforgivable. If that flash of white on the landing had been Lisa, it might well be that she had ventured down from her room out of curiosity, and had come to her own conclusions before her father had had the opportunity to speak to her.

It was, however, useless speculating about the incident, Helen decided after a time as she stretched out a hand to turn off the light and slipped into bed. It was a futile occupation trying to solve problems without knowing the true facts, and she would know soon enough after tomorrow.

CHAPTER THREE

IT was cloudy and cold when Helen arrived at Brock Castle just after two the following day. The sound of the restless ocean was carried towards her on the strong breeze that whipped her skirt against her legs and tugged at the belt of her corduroy jacket and she sped up the steps to the front door and raised the knocker.

She was admitted by the man she had seen before, and he asked politely for the keys to her car, his brown face less severe in the daylight, although his dark glance was intensely curious.

'The master is in his study,' he told her. The message was clear, however. Mr Savage was awaiting her arrival, and she felt rather like a fly that was invited into the spider's web.

Her murmured thanks were lost in a gust of wind before she hurried inside, finding her way without difficulty to the living-room with its drab furnishings. At the study door she hesitated briefly, shivering with slight apprehension, and partly from the cold, but it was too late now to change her mind. Drawing a deep breath to steady her nerves, she raised her hand and knocked before entering.

'So you've arrived, Miss Talbot,' Simon Savage said as he rose from behind the large ebony desk and came towards her. Her hand was temporarily engulfed in his before he indicated brusquely that she should sit down. 'I must say I doubted whether you would have the nerve to go through with it, and I actually expected a telephone call to say that you'd changed your mind.'

Helen seated herself on the uncomfortable straight-backed chair which she remembered from the evening before, and her hands automatically sought the familiarity of the carved wooden arms. 'I don't usually make rash decisions, only to back out at the last minute.'

'Meaning that this was a rash decision, and that your pride wouldn't let you retract your application?'

'Meaning nothing of the sort!' she retaliated just as swiftly as the question had been shot at her, and well aware that she had stepped neatly into the trap.

'But you did nurture a few doubts as to the wisdom of your decision,' he persisted, his rugged features equally harsh in the cold light of day, although his scarred cheek appeared less frightening than it had the night before.

'To doubt is a natural reaction, surely?'

'Natural and logical when you stop to consider what you're letting yourself in for.'

The firmly chiselled lips twisted into a semblance of a smile that never quite reached the dark intensity of his eyes as they flicked over her person. Helen withstood his glance a moment longer until a pulse fluttered strangely in her throat, forcing her to lower her lashes to avoid those relentlessly probing eyes.

'Mr Savage, I have the strangest feeling that you're trying to make me change my mind,' she broke the silence in a voice that was not quite steady.

Her observation appeared to amuse him, for strong white teeth flashed against the tan of his features as he leaned back against his desk and folded his arms across his chest. 'Perhaps I am.'

'Why?'

His glance travelled slowly and deliberately from her silvery head down to her feet. 'I've only just realised how very young you are, and how vulnerable you would be to the village gossipers.'

'You weren't too concerned about that last night,' she recalled, raising her glance no higher than the rolled collar of his thick woollen sweater.

'No,' he admitted, extending his cigarette case towards her and, when she refused, lighting one for himself. 'But I, too, have been doubting the good sense of my actions. I'm not exactly in my dotage, Miss Talbot. I'm thirty-five, and still young enough to appreciate a beautiful woman; a woman with a classic beauty such as yours, for instance.' His eyes mocked her through a screen of smoke. 'Do you understand what I'm trying to say?'

'Yes.' The colour rose in her cheeks as she held his glance unwaveringly. 'The villagers will naturally think the worst.'

'Exactly,' he said harshly, moving away from her to stare out of the window, but his expression relayed such bitterness that Helen felt as though her heart had been clamped in a vice.

'Would it trouble you?' she asked, keeping her eyes riveted to the books stacked neatly in the shelves against the opposite wall. Some of them were leather-bound volumes containing the works of J. B. Priestley, Aristotle, Shakespeare and Yeats. A curious assortment, she thought humorously as she looked up to find him standing beside her chair.

'Many things have been said about me in the past, Miss Talbot, so what difference would one or two added accusations make to the long list I've already acquired?'

'Then the matter is settled, don't you think?'

'Be it on your own head, but don't say that I didn't give you adequate warning.'

His voice was gratingly harsh while his thunderous eyes sent an involuntary shiver through her. There was an unflexible hardness about him that made Helen wonder if he would ever be capable of harbouring any tender emotions. A curious thought to be contemplating at that moment, she realised with a measure of shock, but one that lingered uncomfortably as she watched him draw hard on his cigarette and flick the remainder into the fire.

The strained silence was interrupted by a light tap on the door, and Simon Savage frowned heavily. 'Come in.'

A young Coloured woman entered, her long black hair hanging in a neat plait down her back, and her white overall spotless. Her almond-coloured eyes darted with swift curiosity in Helen's direction before she glanced apologetically at the man who stood frowning down at her.

'I'm sorry, Master Simon,' she said, wringing her hands together in a gesture that indicated she was troubled, 'but Missie Lisa is not in her room.'

Helen held her breath unconsciously as Simon demanded, 'Then where the devil is she?'

'I don't know, Master Simon,' the woman owned, the slightly full lips quivering in her brown face. 'I've searched through all the rooms, and Jacob and Rosie are busy searching the garden now.'

'Have you looked up on the turret?'

'Yes, Master Simon,' the dark head nodded agitatedly. 'I left her ten minutes ago playing in her room, but when I went up to her again, she was gone.'

'I wonder what the devil that child thinks she's playing at,' he demanded furiously from no one in particular, his anger evident in the way he clenched his hands at his sides, and the livid redness of the scar on his cheek. 'She knew I'd be taking you up to meet her.'

'Perhaps that's the reason for her disappearance,' Helen offered tentatively, making an effort to save the explosive situation. 'Children are inclined to be nervous and shy when they have to meet strangers.'

'She deliberately disobeyed my instructions,' he insisted, turning sharply to the woman who had stood listening to their discourse in wary silence. 'Bella, I suggest you help with the search outside while I go through the house once more.'

Bella, as Helen now knew her name to be, nodded silently and left the study with a swish of starched material, and moments later they heard the outer door being closed.

'Mr Savage,' Helen began hesitantly as he was about to

begin with another search of the house, 'please don't be too harsh on Lisa. It would only make her dislike me before we've had the opportunity to meet.'

His broad shoulders moved slightly beneath his sweater while his entire attitude conveyed disapproval—of her, of Lisa, and the entire situation. The tightness about his lips did not relax as he said stiffly: 'She deserves to be punished.'

'Overlook it just this once, Mr Savage . . . please?'

Helen had risen to her feet as she spoke, no longer wishing to suffer the disadvantage of having to crane her neck to look up at him, but trembling with apprehension at her temerity to plead so persistently for his small daughter.

For one frightened moment she expected the lash of his tongue, then his harsh features appeared to relax slightly. 'It would appear that, without realising it, Lisa has found a champion in you, Miss Talbot.'

It wa a cutting remark, tinged with mockery, but Helen continued undaunted, 'To punish her now would only jeopardise the relationship between your daughter and myself, and it would make my task so much more difficult. You *must* realise that?'

The wind rattled the windows in protest, the fierce elements of nature matching the stormy atmosphere in this small room that served as a study.

'Very well, Miss Talbot,' he said at length, thrusting his hands into the pockets of his brown slacks. 'Just this once I shall ignore her behaviour, but if her disobedience continues, I shall have no hesitation in punishing her as she deserves.'

Helen expelled the air carefully from her lungs, realising for the first time how tensely she had been awaiting his reply. 'Thank you.'

The door opened unexpectedly and Bella entered, almost dragging a small child by the hand. 'We found her hiding in the old garden shed, Master Simon.'

'Thank you, Bella. You may go.'

The door closed behind her slightly plump figure, and Helen's heart contracted with sympathy for the child who stood cowering back against the wall. Straight dark hair, similar to that of her father, hung down to her shoulders, while her dark brown eyes were two large pools of fear in a heart-shaped face that looked pale and pinched. Her hands tugged relentlessly at the green sweater she wore over her woollen slacks, while her eyes darted nervously about the room as if in search of escape.

'Come here, Lisa.' A pink lower lip trembled, but she obeyed nevertheless to stand before her father with her head lowered. 'I want you to meet your new governess. Miss Talbot, this is my daughter Lisa.' A firm hand propelled the child forward. 'Say "how do you do", Lisa.'

The child stumbled through the stiff formality of the greeting, bringing a lump to Helen's throat as she clasped the small hand extended towards her and felt the nervous twitching of the fingers against her palm.

Her softly spoken, 'Hello, Lisa. I've been looking forward to meeting you,' was lost on the child in the tense atmosphere that prevailed, and she could not help wishing that she had been allowed to meet Lisa in different circumstances—and alone!

'Can I go to my room now?' Lisa asked in a squeaky little voice, and the tall, silent man leaning against the desk met Helen's glance with a hint of exasperation in the depths of his dark eyes.

'Yes, you may go,' he said to his daughter, raising a warning finger. 'But no more tricks. Understand?'

Lisa nodded slowly and, darting a frightened glance over her shoulder, she left the study as swiftly as she could.

Helen felt pitifully sorry for her at that moment as she sent a thankful glance in her employer's direction, but he was staring fixedly at the carpet, oblivious of her presence

for the moment. Her arrival at Brock Castle had succeeded
in causing a minor upset, she thought sadly, and the incident had made her decidedly edgy and doubtful of her
capabilities.

'I was going to discuss your duties with you, but I think
it would be better if I showed you to your suite and allowed
you to settle in first,' Simon Savage said as he emerged
from his thoughtful pose and opened the study door. 'Our
discussion will have to be postponed until after dinner.'

He led the way through the large entrance hall where a
stinkwood chest appeared to dominate the one wall, while
two straight-backed chairs, with strips of hide interwoven
across the seats, were placed on either side of the chest. The
heavy suit of armour, left by the family of the original
owners to become part of the Castle, stood in the corner
nearest the front door, and looked just as solid and dependable as on the first occasion Helen had admired it several
years ago.

She was acutely conscious of the lithe figure beside her as
they went up the darkened stairs to the upper floor. His
silence completely unnerved her, just as the light touch of
his guiding hand at her elbow sparked off an awareness that
was similar to an electric current. She would have to be
careful, she told herself wryly, or she might find herself up
against a force far stronger than she was able to cope with.

She followed him down the gloomy passage until he
stopped abruptly and opened a door. As he stood aside for
her to enter, she brushed past him and became aware of the
faint odour of tobacco and shaving cream; a peculiar blend
that was somehow pleasing to the senses.

Pulling herself together sharply, she realised that she was
standing in a small but comfortably furnished lounge which
was part of the suite she was to occupy during her stay at
Brock Castle. Compared with the living-room downstairs,
this room was like a bright oasis. The chairs were covered
in a soft, cream-coloured fabric, with a cool blue carpet to

set them off, and in the small stone fireplace the logs were packed, ready to be lit that evening.

Simon Savage's presence seemed to dominate the room, and her senses, as he indicated which rooms were hers. She would, she decided, examine them at her leisure afterwards, and preferably without those disturbing eyes following her about.

'That's Lisa's room,' he told her, gesturing towards the door leading off to the right as he prepared to leave. 'I hope you'll find everything satisfactory.'

Helen was certain that he cared very little whether she found everything satisfactory or not, for his expressionless face indicated that his thoughts were already elsewhere and not at all with the woman he had just employed to take care of his child.

'By the way,' he said, turning back to her, 'dinner is at six-thirty precisely. Lisa will show you the way to the dining-room, if you think you might not find your way on your own.'

The door closed behind him before she could think of an appropriate reply, and she was alone suddenly in unfamiliar surroundings, with a child in the adjoining room who had not the slightest interest in her new governess, and whose confidence would have to be cultivated with the greatest care.

Curious to know what the rest of the suite looked like, Helen went through to the bedroom and removed her jacket as she glanced about her in surprise. The furnishings were of a soft rose-pink, while the polished brass bed had a lace bedspread of similar colour thrown over it.

She hesitated momentarily in front of the full-length mirror, appalled at her windswept appearance. Her silvery fair hair, which had so often caused comment because of its unusual colour, hung untidily about her shoulders. Blue, heavily lashed eyes gazed warily back at her beneath finely arched brows, while the generous curve of her lips quivered into a derisive smile.

'You've certainly rushed in where others have feared to tread,' she scolded herself. 'Let's hope you don't regret it, or everyone will find great pleasure in saying, "I told you so"!'

Her suitcases had been placed neatly beside the wardrobe, and Helen opened the first one, taking her time to unpack as she contemplated the strong possibility that there would be nothing to do and no one to talk to during the hours before dinner.

Acting on an impulse, she left her bedroom door slightly ajar, hoping that Lisa might display the same curiosity as she had done the evening before, and, not long afterwards, her assumption proved correct. She was being carefully observed through the crevice in the door and, pretending that she was unaware of this, she continued with her task, but she could not prevent the quiver of excitement that went through her. Lisa's curiosity was a healthy sign, and, glancing into her suitcase, Helen thought of a possible way to entice her out into the open.

She took out the small musical jewellery box and held it in her hands for a moment, fingering the delicately carved oriental motifs on the ivory lid. It had belonged to her mother—a memento of their trip to the East. The small watching figure became statue-like, her attention supposedly captured by the unusual item, and Helen smiled to herself as she lifted the lid and allowed the tinkling, typically Eastern music to fill the room.

Lisa let out a soft yet audible gasp, but Helen pretended not to hear as she allowed the music to play on until it had wound down completely. Helen's fingers sought the key, but she refrained from turning it as she silently willed the child to show herself, and, when it finally became apparent that her ruse had failed, she sighed, placing the box carefully on the dressing-table.

When the last suitcase was stowed away on top of the wardrobe, Helen noticed that Lisa had gone, and she could only conclude that Lisa had anticipated the fact that she might be discovered at any moment, therefore she had returned to her own room as silently as she had left it.

Helen went through to the bathroom to freshen up, only vaguely aware of the gleaming white tiles and rose-pink towels as she made up her mind to pay Lisa a visit. She brushed her hair vigorously to restore some life to it, and touched up her lipstick, then, satisfied with her appearance, she left her bedroom and crossed the small lounge.

Lisa was lying on her bed with a picture book resting on her raised knees, but, as Helen knocked briefly on the door and entered, she threw the book aside and slid nervously off the bed to stand beside it with a guilty look in her lowered eyes. The reason for her guilt was vaguely puzzling to Helen—unless the child suspected that she had been seen when she had stood peeping through the crevice in the door?

'Hello, Lisa,' Helen smiled tentatively, deciding not to mention the fact that she had known of her presence. 'I hope you don't mind my coming into your room like this, but it's rather lonely with no one to talk to.'

She gestured that the child should lie down once more, but Lisa remained standing rigidly beside the bed, and Helen, after searching for a chair and finding none, seated herself gingerly on the edge of Lisa's bed as she met the child's suspicious glance.

'Have you been reading this?' Helen asked casually, picking up the book and discovering that it was a generally informative book on the various breeds of dogs, and specially compiled for children of Lisa's age. Grasping at this topic as a starting point to break through the barrier the child had erected between them, Helen asked: 'Do you like dogs?'

Those brown eyes remained watchful and suspicious,

although the dark head nodded perceptibly.

'I had a dog once,' Helen told her, trying to ignore the lack of response and behaving as naturally as possible. 'I called him Spats because he was brown with white paws.' Lisa stared at her blankly. 'Do you know what spats are?'

Lisa gestured negatively with her head and Helen explained. 'Years ago it was the fashion for men to wear white gaiters, a sort of cloth, over the instep of their shoes, and it used to reach up to their ankles. They were called spats.'

There was no response in the pinched little face and Helen tried again. 'Do you have any friends who come to play?'

'Daddy won't allow me to have any friends.'

Helen's heart leapt at this verbal response, but the flicker of fear in the child's eyes disturbed her immensely.

'Why not, Lisa?' A pink lower lip trembled and Helen thought it best not to pursue the subject. 'Do you like school?'

'No.'

Once again there was that look of fear that seemed to tear at Helen's heart. 'It can be fun if you make it so.'

Lisa did not reply, but lowered her head and stared sullenly at the carpet, moving the toe of her shoe along the flowery patterns.

Taking this opportunity to glance about her, Helen noticed that the room was rather small, and done out in white with pale lemon curtains and bedspread. There was a white chest of drawers with polished brass handles, and a wardrobe to match. Other than that there was a small white table beside the bed, and a square chest which possibly contained her toys.

The wind grew stronger, but it carried with it the sound of the angry waves. 'Can you hear the sea above the wind?' she asked Lisa. 'When I was a little girl I used to love walking on the beach when it had become too cold to swim during the winter months.'

Lisa watched her intently, but said nothing. There was, however, a strong resemblance to her father in the way she held her head, and Helen's pulse leapt irrationally at this discovery.

'There's a cave in the rocks along this beach and, unless someone else has discovered it, it's still my very own secret place where I used to go when I wanted to be alone.' There was a flicker of interest in Lisa's eyes that encouraged Helen to continue. 'If you like, I'll take you there one day when the weather is warmer.'

Lisa did not appear to be interested in her suggestion and, disappointed, Helen rose to return to her room. 'I'll leave you now to get on with your reading.'

At the door she hesitated, but the child had not stirred except for those large brown eyes following her departing figure.

Grasping at Simon's statement earlier that afternoon, she turned and said: 'Wait for me when it's time to go down to dinner. I'm not so sure that I'll find my way. Will you wait?'

'Yes,' the reply came after a moment's hesitation, and Helen felt the tension uncoil within her.

'Thank you, Lisa,' she smiled briefly. 'I'll see you later, then.'

The dining-room, Helen discovered that evening, was the only room where the yellow-wood floor had been preserved and waxed to a high sheen, and it had been left bare except for a small rug in the centre of the room. It was not as drably furnished as the living-room, but the heavy dark green curtains gave it the same depressing atmosphere.

Although she had changed into a fresh skirt and blouse before venturing downstairs, she soon realised that, despite the glittering formality of the silverware, her employer obviously cared little for the idea of dressing for dinner. Helen was secretly overjoyed by the casual informality of

Simon Savage's household, for her one evening dress would not have been adequate had circumstances been different.

Lisa had waited, as Helen had asked her to, but she had maintained her obstinate silence as they made their way down to the dining-room. It was a strange experience sitting through a silent dinner with her employer and his daughter, for they were both equally remote and sullen. It was a far cry from the chatty meals shared with her aunt in the cosy atmosphere of her bright little kitchen, she thought, feeling a little depressed.

Bella appeared as Lisa drained her glass of milk, and the child allowed herself to be led willingly enough up to her room. Helen wished desperately that she could have followed her, but her employer had mentioned that he wished to discuss her duties with her, and so she remained seated, her hands clasped tightly in her lap as she waited.

The wind had been increasing in velocity all afternoon, and Helen shivered involuntarily as she thought of the storm that would inevitably follow. Dark eyes observed her reaction with cynical amusement, placing her instantly on the defensive and awakening a slumbering antagonism.

'Do these coastal storms frighten you?'

'Not particularly,' she replied, avoiding his glance. 'But I know the damage they can do.'

'Damage?' he queried sharply.

'The wind has, in the past, caused severe damage to several houses, and the rain, on one occasion, practically washed the foundations out from under some of those cottages higher up on the hill. Small children, playing in the path of the flood, would have drowned had the lumberjacks not rushed down the hill with their timely warning.' Helen experienced again that familiar chill of fear as she recalled these incidents. 'The stream, which runs through a section of the village, overflowed its banks that day and several houses had to be evacuated.'

'I presume this doesn't happen often?'

Helen shook her head. 'No, not often, but when it does, everyone in the village lends a hand, and the church hall becomes a sanctuary as well as a temporary hospital if there are injuries to be attended to.'

'You have obviously lived through one of those storms,' he remarked, and, as she raised her glance, she noticed that he had a peculiar twist to his lips which gave him a slightly satanic expression.

'Two of them, to be exact,' she replied quietly.

His expression became remote once more, and Helen became aware, for the first time, of the fine network of scars on the back of his left hand as he lit a cigarette.

'About Lisa,' he said, suddenly businesslike. 'I would prefer it if you kept everything to a strict routine by starting with her lessons at eight in the morning. Your tea will be brought up to you at ten-thirty precisely, and the lessons may then continue until twelve-thirty. After lunch she is to rest for an hour, and how you occupy yourselves after that is not particularly my concern.'

'As long as she's kept out of your way,' Helen thought caustically, but instead, taking his lengthy silence as an indication that he had said all that he intended to say, she rose to her feet and said: 'Very well, Mr Savage. If that's all, then I think I'll go up to my room.'

'Kindly sit down, I haven't finished yet.'

His voice held a note of authority, and she resumed her seat instantly, lowering her head and allowing her hair to fall forward in an effort to hide her flushed cheeks. 'I'm sorry.'

'You will have breakfast and lunch in your rooms with Lisa,' he continued unperturbed. 'I have breakfast very early, and usually have a sandwich in my study at lunchtime. The evening meal we naturally all have together.' He drew hard on his cigarette and leaned back in his chair. 'Any questions?'

Helen pulled herself together. 'Where are these lessons to take place?'

'The room opposite yours has been furnished specifically for this purpose. You'll find everything you require in the wall-cupboard, but if there should be anything else you may need, then I trust you'll let me know?' His tight-lipped expression relaxed slightly. 'I also want a daily report on her progress. Perhaps after dinner in the evenings will be a suitable time.'

This was the most ridiculous suggestion Helen had ever heard of, but, for the time being, she refrained from telling him so.

'There is one other thing,' he continued with a certain amount of urgency in the way he sat forward in his chair and held her glance. 'She's not to run at will through the grounds without being accompanied by an adult, preferably yourself. There are certain sections to the northern and eastern side of the grounds that haven't been cleared as yet, and the possibility of snakes can't be ruled out. You are now responsible for Lisa, and I expect you to discipline her where necessary. And, unless it's absolutely necessary, I'm not to be disturbed in my study.'

What could be of such importance that he would not want to be disturbed unnecessarily? she wondered, and then, quite suddenly, she stared at him in a flash of stunning recognition. How *stupid* of her not to have realised it sooner! He was none other than the famous South African playwright, whose works had been produced and acclaimed so highly in this country, as well as overseas during the past few years ... and she was now in his employ!

'You've gone quite pale, Miss Talbot,' his deep voice penetrated her confused thoughts. 'Are you feeling ill?'

'No, I—I've just realised who you are,' she stammered out the truth, clutching at her chair with both hands as if she expected it to give way beneath her.

'Really?'

His expression became veiled and dangerously bored, but she rushed into speech without taking much care in choosing her words. 'I was at the opening night of your play in Cape Town last year. That was *The Truth About Emma Jones*, I think. The critics like it,' she ended lamely.

'But *you* didn't,' he guessed accurately, his eyes flaming with mockery.

'I—well, I——'

'Please feel free to speak your mind, Miss Talbot,' he invited, not without a certain amount of condescension. 'It should be quite interesting to learn what one of the general public thinks of my work.'

Helen knew that she had been placed cleverly in a category where her inexperienced and unauthorised opinion was actually of no importance in the literary sense, but, partly because of his attitude, and partly because of a deep-rooted anger within her, she stated her opinion with a boldness she was far from experiencing.

'I found that you had created characters who were coldly calculating when it came to the human aspects of life.'

'Did you really? Why?'

'They lacked the usual warmth in their relationships, and the ability to care about the problems of other people.'

Simon Savage put out his cigarette and held her glance with amused interest. 'You sound like a romantic, Miss Talbot.'

Helen wished feverishly that she had not allowed herself to become involved in a discussion of this nature with her employer, but it was too late to alter the situation. 'Most people are romantics to a certain extent, I think.'

'Then most people are foolishly walking with their heads in the clouds, and living in a world of fantasy,' he lashed out severely, the expression on his scarred face frightening to observe. 'The reality of life is harsh, often cruel, and there's no escaping the nettles that come your way. There's passion, hate and suffering, and we are all basically geared to trample someone under our feet when we want something badly enough. People lie and cheat to gain their own objectives. They play on your feelings as one would pluck the strings of a harp, then, when they've got what they want, you're discarded like a piece of flotsam. Women,' he added savagely, 'are especially good at that sort of thing.'

Helen stared at him speechlessly for a moment. Never before had she encountered such a storm of bitterness emanating from one person, and the discovery left her feeling curiously drained.

'We're all entitled to our own opinions, Mr Savage, but I think I would rather be a romantic than a cynic,' she informed him with an unusual mixture of pity and anger.

His lips twisted slightly. 'I'm a cynic, Miss Talbot, because life has proved to me that I'm right.'

'I hope you don't intend to coach your daughter into believing as you yourself do?' she retorted with growing antagonism.

'Lisa will be free to make her own observations, and I dare say she's already reached a few similar conclusions.'

He rose to his feet and Helen followed his example, facing him unflinchingly with her head thrown back to reveal the graceful curve of her neck where the rapid beat of a tiny pulse was the only evidence of her agitation.

'Then it will be my task to enlighten her to the contrary,' her voice rang out above the noise of the wind.

'Or to teach her the devious wiles so frequently employed by women,' he shot back at her, his probing glance finding that agitated pulse at the base of her throat, and lingering accusingly.

Helen's hand flew to her throat and, with a murmured 'goodnight', she fled up to her room. Simon Savage did not try to follow her, nor to prevent her departure, but, when she closed the door of her suite behind her, she leaned against it for several seconds in an effort to catch her breath.

'What's the matter with me?' she asked herself angrily. 'Why do I allow him to upset me in this way? What do I care about his opinions and how he chooses to live his life? I'm here to teach and guide his daughter until she's well enough to return to school, nothing more!'

Within a few months, if she was successful in remaining longer than her predecessors, she would be leaving Brock Castle in the same manner as she had arrived. Her task would have been completed and, as it was unlikely that their paths would ever cross again, she could just forget about him.

Forget about him, she repeated her thoughts, but Simon Savage was not a man who could be forgotten with ease. One does not forget easily that one has been scorched by a smouldering fire.

Helen was awakened in the night by the violence of the storm, but it was not the sound of the rain lashing against her window or the electrifying clap of thunder that held her attention. The frightened whimpering of a child made her reach for her robe and slip her feet into the soft mules beside her bed.

Thankful now that she had thought to open Lisa's door before going to bed, she crossed the darkened lounge swiftly and entered the child's room.

'Lisa?'

The whimpering was instantly stifled, and Helen went forward quickly to snap on the bedside light. 'Does the storm frighten you?'

Lisa shook her head and cowered back against the pillows, but her pale, tear-stained cheeks, and the hands clutching nervously at the sheets told their own story. A crackling flash of lightning was followed by an earth-shattering clap of thunder, making the child cringe visibly, and Helen's tender heart could take no more. Without a moment's hesitation she sat down on the side of the bed and scooped the frightened child into her arms.

Lisa buried her face without protest against the comfortable hollow of Helen's shoulder, her hands clutching desperately at the blue candlewick robe as the reassuring strength of slender arms tightened about her trembling form. Helen laid her cheek against Lisa's dark head and spoke soothingly to her as the storm continued to rage outside.

As time elapsed, Lisa's trembling ceased until she finally fell asleep with a small hand beneath a rosy cheek against Helen's breast. A gentle smile curved Helen's lips as she observed the sleeping child, moving her arms slightly to ease the muscles that were aching in protest against the unaccustomed weight. Loath to leave her in these circumstances, but finding it increasingly difficult to keep awake, Helen eased herself on to the bed and, covering them both with the rug, she promptly went to sleep with Lisa lying more comfortably in her arms.

How long she slept like that she could not be sure, but she awoke to the alarming discovery that the storm had subsided to a steady downpour, and that Simon Savage was bending over her. Confused, she blinked up at him for a moment before she eased her arm gently from beneath Lisa's sleeping form, but the movement parted the front of her robe and revealed the seductive curve of breasts only partially concealed by the transparent lace of her nightgown.

With rapidly beating heart Helen dragged the two sections of her robe together, but from the sudden quirk of his lips she knew that her action had been too late. Embarrassment sent the colour surging from her throat into her cheeks, and, refusing to meet his glance, she slipped off the bed and stood poised for flight on the carpet before him.

He exuded a savage masculinity in his brown silk dressing-gown which was parted to reveal the shadow of hair on his tanned chest, and also the fact that he slept only in pyjama trousers. Helen observed him beneath lowered lashes, his tall presence sparking off an awareness that attacked her senses in a way that made her conscious for the first time of her femininity. It was an experience that was totally foreign to her, and wild panic rose in her throat as she realised what a fool she had been not to heed the warnings of her aunt, and Simon Savage himself. He was far too dangerous a man to live with under one roof without experiencing some sort of emotional impact.

'You'd better get back to your bed,' he dismissed her in a lowered voice. 'The storm is over, and you're shivering with the cold.'

Helen turned to leave, surprised to discover that she was trembling, not shivering, but somehow she reached the door without her legs giving way beneath her.

'Miss Talbot?' She gripped the side of the door and glanced back with some trepidation to see him raking a hand through his dark hair. 'I appreciate what you did for Lisa. If I hadn't been in such a dead sleep, I would have helped her myself.'

Astonished at this disclosure, Helen merely nodded and made her way back to her own bed. It was some time before she went to sleep again, and then her dreams were haunted by the menacing figure of her employer bearing down on her. Her desperate search for escape was thwarted by some strange magnetic power he had exerted over her, and, when it seemed that her capture was inevitable, she awoke with a cry to find herself sitting upright in bed. Relieved and exhausted, she fell back against the pillows and, as her pulse resumed its regular pace, she finally slipped into a dreamless state of oblivion.

CHAPTER FOUR

HELEN awoke on Sunday morning and stretched lazily as she toyed with the idea of remaining in bed a little longer, then, as she recalled the storm during the night, she realised where she was. She raised a languid arm and glanced at her wrist watch. Six-thirty. It was still early, but not being familiar with the household routine at Brock Castle, she slipped out of bed and pulled on her robe.

How would Lisa react when they met again? she wondered curiously as she went through to the bathroom. Would she be more withdrawn simply because she had been forced to seek comfort from someone she still distrusted, or would she be a little more forthcoming?

When Helen finally returned to her room, there was a knock on her door and Bella entered with a tray of coffee.

'Good morning, madam,' she said politely, placing the tray on the bedside table. 'I thought the madam would still be asleep.'

'I wouldn't want to be caught napping on my first morning her,' Helen told her, sitting down on the side of the bed and helping herself to the steaming coffee. 'Hm, this tastes good!'

'No one gets up before seven in this house,' Bella informed her, hovering at the foot of the bed and displaying a curious reluctance to leave. Her almond eyes observed Helen closely for a moment before a smile of approval creased her brown face. 'The madam will be good for my Missie Lisa.'

It was not a question, but a statement, and, although it surprised Helen, it gave her a peculiar feeling of satisfaction to know that someone, at least, had confidence in her. 'You're obviously very fond of Lisa.'

'I have looked after her since she was a baby,' Bella
announced proudly. 'Her mother...' She hesitated, awakening Helen's curiosity, then she changed the subject abruptly. 'Missie Lisa told me that you went to her in the
night.'

'Did she sound upset about it?' Helen asked carefully.

'No, madam. She just said that the madam hadn't been
angry with her for being frightened,' came the prompt
reply.

'Why should I have been angry?' Helen asked in surprise
as she recalled the pathetic little figure cringing away at the
sound of the storm.

Bella shifted her weight uncomfortably from one foot to
the other before she replied. 'It's not my place to talk, but
the other governesses never understood Missie Lisa's behaviour. She has not been well, and she frightens easily, but
Master Simon had said that they mustn't pamper her.
Missie Lisa needs a lot of love, I always tell Jacob—that's
my husband—and love is something she has never had
much of in the past.'

'Master S-Simon,' Helen stumbled slightly over the
name. 'Doesn't he give her a lot of love and attention?'

Bella's face clouded. 'Master Simon is always busy writing. He wouldn't want anything to make her unhappy, but
his heart is like a stone.'

His heart is like a stone. The words seemed to echo
through her mind long after Bella had gone. It was an
indisputable fact, she thought unkindly. He might just as
well have been chiselled out of granite, for she could not
imagine him displaying any of the warm and tender emotions which were such basic ingredients with most people.
He had a very low opinion of the human race in general,
and women specifically, she had discovered during their
discussion the previous evening.

This harsh quality was evident in his plays as well, she

thought, recalling the night she had gone to see *The Truth About Emma Jones*. His wife, Brenda Allen, had played the leading role; the last leading role in any play before her untimely death. Her dark beauty had captivated the audience, and her acting had been superb, but Helen had left the theatre in a distraught state of mind, unable to believe that anyone could have created characters such as those she had just seen. They had loved and hated passionately, but the thread of cruelty had wound its way throughout the entire play with never a moment of tenderness to warm the heart as each character displayed a vicious destructiveness in the mad scramble for personal success.

A sigh escaped Helen as she glanced at the time. What purpose was there in wasting time trying to analyse a man as complex as her employer? His bitterness at the loss of his wife and son was understandable, but why should that bitterness against life itself have been so evident before that fatal accident? He must have known *some* happiness with his wife and children?

The clouds were dispersing and the sun was putting in an appearance, she noticed as she stared out of her window, allowing her glance to stray across the outbuildings and the bushy sand dunes, to the great expanse of the Indian Ocean beyond. It looked so peaceful, but deceptively so, for its murky appearance in places indicated a turbulence beneath the surface; a turbulence she was just as aware of within herself.

Brushing aside her thoughts irritably, she opened her wardrobe and pulled out a comfortable pair of slacks and thick sweater. After the storm the previous night they could expect a chilly day, she decided as she dressed quickly. Her entrance into her private lounge, some minutes later, could not have been timed better, for it coincided with Bella's.

'Your breakfast, madam,' she smiled politely, placing a tray on the low coffee table.

'Good heavens!' Helen exclaimed with a touch of humour as she lifted the lid of the dish and sniffed appreciatively at the aroma of fried eggs, bacon done to a crisp, and toast. 'I can't possibly eat all this!'

Bella's glance assessed Helen's slenderness beneath the bulky sweater, and she smiled benignly. 'Rosie made the breakfast. She said the madam was skin and bone, like someone who had been starving.'

'*Did* she now,' Helen laughed good-naturedly, raising a hand without thinking and fingering the hollows in her cheeks. She *had* lost weight during the past year, but not to the extent Rosie had implied. 'Tell Rosie I shall do my best with the lovely meal she's provided.'

Bella smiled with satisfaction as she returned to the kitchen, leaving Helen to struggle through the enormous breakfast Rosie had prepared as a start to the fattening-up process.

A slight movement caught her eye, and she raised her glance to smile at the child who stood observing her with a frown of concentration puckering her brow.

'Good morning, Lisa. Have you had breakfast?'

Lisa nodded and stepped back a pace.

'Then do come and keep me company while I have mine,' Helen suggested persuasively, holding her breath for an instant when it appeared as though Lisa would dart back into her room, but her expressive little face relaxed slightly and she came forward slowly to seat herself on the edge of the chair opposite Helen.

Pretending that the incident during the night had not occurred, Helen managed to maintain a casual air as she finished her breakfast and helped herself to a cup of coffee. 'You have lovely hair, Lisa. Does Bella brush it for you?'

'Yes,' Lisa replied with a slight lisp as she nervously clutched her hands together in her lap. 'Sometimes I brush it myself.'

Although encouraged by the response she was receiving, Helen employed just as much care as she had done before in drawing her out. 'Would you like to share this slice of toast with me? I really can't finish it all.'

'Thank you,' Lisa murmured shyly as she helped herself to the toast which Helen offered her, but she continued to observe Helen closely for several seconds before she asked: 'What's your name?'

Helen's heart lurched hopefully as she supplied her name.

'Helen,' Lisa repeated slowly, and with careful thought. 'It's a nice name.'

'You may call me Helen, if you like,' she told the child, and was rewarded by a flicker of friendly warmth in the brown depths of those large eyes. Dabbing at her lips with the table napkin, Helen asked: 'What are we going to do today?'

'I don't know.'

'Well, if you want to, you could show me where you will have your lessons, then we could go exploring in the garden.' She cast a swift glance at the window. 'The weather looks promising, and it might be fun.'

Lisa frowned. 'What's exploring?'

'It means to examine. Look at, if you like,' Helen explained briefly.

'There's nothing much in the garden to look at.'

'Oh, but there could be if you know what to look for,' Helen protested gently. 'Shall we take this tray down to the kitchen first?'

Lisa shook her head. 'You don't have to do that. Bella always takes it down when she comes in to tidy up.'

'All right, then. Shall we go?' Helen suggested, rising to her feet and giving herself a timid mental pat on the shoulder.

'This is where I have my lessons,' Lisa told her, opening the door opposite hers in the passage.

'How lovely,' Helen remarked enthusiastically as she glanced about the spacious room done out in avocado green and white. It was a miniature classroom with a table and chair for her own use, as well as a small desk for Lisa. A blackboard had been erected against the wall behind the table, and bookshelves, containing enough reading matter for an entire school, lined another wall. The large window gave one an excellent view of the hills with their yellow-wood and stinkwood plantations, while the early morning sun shed its rays into the room to fill it with a glowing warmth.

Helen glanced down at her small companion. 'It must be wonderful to work in a room as lovely as this.'

'I don't like school,' Lisa muttered.

'Why not?'

Lisa shrugged and scowled at the floor. 'It makes me tired.'

Helen's glance softened instantly as she made a mental note not to overtax the child's strength too much at first. 'Let's go for that walk in the garden.'

Helen kept to the gravel path among the dense foliage that formed part of Brock Castle's spacious grounds. To have take any other route would have been foolhardy, for the storm had turned the leafy soil into a spongy carpet which would not be negotiable for several days until the water had drained away sufficiently.

Lisa displayed a complete lack of interest, at first, but Helen's natural enthusiasm for her surroundings finally awakened a flicker of interest in the child. Among other things, they collected leaves of various colours, shapes and sizes, and were fortunate enough to come upon a dove's nest on a low, overhanging branch of an old acacia tree. Helen lifted Lisa to take a peep into it, and she squealed with delight at discovering two newly hatched doves nestling close together in the nest.

'Do you think we could come and have a look at them again tomorrow?' Lisa asked hopefully as Helen lowered her to the ground.

'Yes, of course.'

'Tomorrow morning?'

Helen shook her head firmly. 'We'll come and have a look at them again tomorrow afternoon after you've had your usual nap—and that's a promise.'

Satisfied, Lisa allowed herself to be led further along the path to examine the bark that was peeling off the stem of an old gum tree. 'Are these trees very old?'

Helen nodded, stooping to examine the piece of bark which had come off in Lisa's hand. 'Some of them are older than Brock Castle.'

'Why is the house called Brock Castle?'

'Well, first of all, because it looks like a castle with its two tall turrets on the east and west side of the house. The one is purely ornamental, as you know, but one can climb to the top of the east tower and have an excellent view of the sea and the hills.'

'How do you know that?'

'I came to Brock Castle once long ago, and I remember being taken on to the turret,' Helen smiled, seating herself on the broad stem of a tree which had been uprooted some years ago to form a natural bench beside the path. 'The actual name "Brock Castle" happened over a long period of time. Would you like to hear about it?'

Lisa shrugged carelessly, but joined Helen on the tree stump all the same, her collection of leaves carefully grouped together in her hands.

'A Mr and Mrs Brock came out to South Africa many years ago, and they had this house built because Mr Brock was a very sick man and he needed to live where there was plenty of sunshine and fresh sea air.' Helen glanced at her small companion surreptitiously and, noticing that she had her complete attention, she continued. 'The people in the village spoke of it as Mr and Mrs Brock's castle, and gradually shortened it to, the Brocks' castle, until it was finally called just Brock Castle. Other people have lived in it since then, and the name was so much a part of the old house that one of the new owners had a brass plaque engraved with the name of it and had it fastened to the gate post.'

'A very interesting story, and one I was not aware of,' a deep voice mocked, and both Lisa and Helen jumped with fright. 'How old do you think Brock Castle is?'

Helen's mind went completely blank for a moment as she stared up at her employer and tried to control the frightened beat of her heart. His faded denims were tucked into muddy boots, and the thick sweater accentuated the broadness of his shoulders as he stood observing her with his head tilted arrogantly, and his thumbs hooked into the heavy belt spanning his slim hips.

'I think it was built approximately eighty years ago,' Helen supplied the answer when she finally found her voice.

'And I dare say that the story concerning the origin of its name has been passed on by word of mouth until there's very little truth in it,' he mocked openly.

Lisa, who had sat silently beside Helen since her father's unexpected arrival, continued her search for leaves in the undergrowth, and appeared quite unperturbed by the antagonistic conversation taking place.

'Mr Perkins, who owns the bakery, told me the story. His father was involved with the building operations at the time, and supplied most of the material,' Helen said stiffly, gesturing towards the house which was only just visible through the trees. 'As you can see, it was built entirely from stones found locally.'

'Then the story must have some truth in it, if Mr Perkins says so,' Simon acknowledged with a twist to his lips.

Why did he have to be so infuriating? she wondered angrily as she rose to her feet and brushed off the seat of her slacks with unsteady hands before following Lisa at a leisurely pace as the child made her way back to the house.

'I'm not a cynic who goes about doubting the word of

those I've known and trusted since childhood,' Helen informed her employer as he fell into step beside her with a grim expression deepening the harsh lines on his face.

'Then you're not only an unusually trusting woman, but also a very naïve one, Miss Talbot. I would take care, though, if I were you. Not everyone can be trusted so implicitly.'

'Do you include yourself in the latter category?' she countered swiftly, and could have bitten off her tongue when the fury of his glance reduced her to an insignificant individual who had had the nerve to question someone like himself.

'When a situation suits my purpose, yes,' he replied in a controlled voice, and then, as Helen was about to follow Lisa's small figure darting along the path towards the house, he gripped her arm. 'Let her go on ahead.'

Helen glanced down at the strong fingers curled about her forearm, and experienced a curious sensation of loss when he released her suddenly.

'I'm glad to see that Lisa has accepted you so quickly,' he remarked in a more natural tone.

'Did you think she wouldn't?'

He shrugged lightly. 'It's difficult to tell with Lisa whether she will react in one way or another. Even at this early age she has all the unpredictable characteristics of a woman.'

If his intention was to anger her, then he was succeeding admirably, Helen thought as she bit back a sharp retort and quickened her pace.

'About last night,' he continued unperturbed. 'I appreciate what you did, but don't make a habit of it. Lisa must learn that she has nothing to fear from these storms.'

'Her fear will diminish in time, but until then, I can't stand by and do nothing to help her. Last night——'

'Last night was exceptional ... and excusable,' he interrupted with flat finality.

Helen stopped in her stride as they reached the edge of the clearing and turned to face him with a defiant tilt to her chin. 'I take it that I *will* have a free hand as far as her education is concerned?'

'Naturally,' his voice grated along her nerves. 'If your methods have the desired results, then I shall leave it to you entirely.'

He inclined his head austerely and set off across the lawn in the opposite direction to the one she was about to take, but Helen reacted with an impulsiveness she regretted afterwards.

'Mr Savage!' she called after him and, when he turned, she took a few uncertain paces towards him. 'You *do* care about Lisa, don't you? I mean ... you do care whether she's happy or not?'

Dark eyes raked her from head to foot with an insolence that sent the blood surging into her cheeks, but somehow she managed to sustain his glance without succumbing to the strong urge to run.

'Miss Talbot, you're forgetting something. Lisa is my daughter, and I have a certain responsibility towards her. If I didn't care about her happiness, I wouldn't have gone through so many governesses in so short a period. I would have kept the first one, and would have allowed Lisa to be frightened into a state where she would have been beyond any psychiatric help.' The muscles in his jaw rippled beneath the scar. 'Does that answer your question?'

Helen licked her lips nervously. 'Yes ... I'm sorry.'

This time he turned on his heel and strode away from her with anger lengthening his stride, but for some minutes she stood staring after him, observing the swing of his shoulders and the way his thick dark hair grew into his neck. Despite the scar on his cheek, he was the most magnificent man she had ever met.

Startled by her own thoughts, she pulled herself together sharply and went in search of Lisa, reprimanding herself at the same time for having had the audacity to question Simon's concern for his small daughter. She had deserved his anger unquestionably, she told herself fiercely.

While Lisa slept that afternoon, Helen took the opportunity to spend an hour in the classroom going through the books Simon had mentioned, and checking on the work Lisa had done previously.

Simon! His dark face forced its way between her and the exercise book she was examining. How easy it had become to think of him in such a familiar way, yet how difficult to believe that there had been a time when his rock-like personality had melted sufficiently in the arms of a woman to produce two children.

The trend of her thoughts made her blush with embarrassment, but a tantalising question arose from it to haunt her. Why was there that undercurrent of hatred within him towards women in general? Or was he merely adopting this attitude towards her, personally, because he feared she might be foolish enough to seek a closer relationship with him?

'Oh, damn the man!' she told herself angrily, banishing him firmly from her mind as she concentrated on the contents of the book before her.

She worked steadily for more than an hour, accepting and rejecting several methods, and making notes as she went along. So absorbed was she in what she was doing that she did not realise how swiftly the time had passed, and she looked up in surprise when Lisa walked in to tell her that Bella had brought a tray of tea up to her room.

Helen's first day at Brock Castle had not been too unsuccessful, she decided some minutes later as she poured tea for Lisa and herself, and sampled the home-made ginger biscuits. Lisa was not very forthcoming about herself as yet, and although she had overcome her initial fear and shyness, she continued to regard Helen with wariness and suspicion. It would take time, Helen realised sadly, to gain Lisa's complete trust. She would have to tread carefully, for there was no way of knowing what reaction she would evoke from a child who tended to flinch at the slightest irregularity in one's voice.

After dinner that evening, Helen went in to say goodnight to Lisa before settling down with a book in front of the fire. The storm clouds had gathered again during the afternoon, and now, as she stood beside Lisa's bed, she could discern flashes of lightning far out to sea. Lisa had seen it as well, for there was a mute appeal in her large eyes which Helen could not ignore despite Simon's warning.

'I'll leave your bedroom door open, and I'll do the same with mine,' Helen told her gently. 'If the storm should come this way during the night and frighten you, will you promise to wake me?'

Lisa chewed at her lip for a moment before she nodded and turned over on to her side, facing the wall. Helen stood watching her for a moment, and then, on an impulse, she leaned over the child and brushed her lips against the soft cheek.

'Goodnight, Lisa.'

She was almost at the door when Lisa's 'Goodnight, Helen,' reached her ears, and a tender smile plucked at her lips.

It was a promising beginning, she told herself as she sat down beside the fire and picked up her book, but why should she feel so tearful about it?

Helen encountered several obstacles during her first week at Brock Castle. The first morning spent in the improvised classroom went off almost too well. Her method of teaching must have appeared strange to Lisa, for she followed Helen's instructions as though it were a game. The bizarre patterns and drawings she had instructed Lisa to make were all part of the specified course Helen intended to follow, and, as she had hoped, Lisa's reluctance to work evaporated as she set to work with her wax crayons.

She was not as successful with Lisa when it came to the actual working subjects, but it was a problem which could be overcome in time when Lisa was more relaxed, and her concentration had improved.

After that first day everything seemed to go wrong. Helen was roused by Lisa's screams most nights, and would rush to her side to calm her down before giving her the tablets Toby had prescribed. They helped considerably, but the nightmares left Lisa feeling washed out and unable to concentrate the following day.

On one occasion Lisa's screams had awakened Simon in his rooms at the other end of the passage, but when he saw that Helen was coping admirably with the situation, he returned to his room, surprisingly enough, without a word.

Confronting Simon each evening with a daily report, was a cumbersome duty while Lisa made no progress at all. He disagreed with her method of teaching, referring back to old-fashioned ideas that were unacceptable to her, and she found herself returning to her suite each evening feeling drained yet triumphant after having been able to convince him that she was correct.

Toby Warren telephoned one afternoon during her second week at Brock Castle, and instead of finding his calm voice reassuring, she felt nervous and irritated.

'When are you going to let me take you out to dinner?' he demanded almost immediately.

'I don't know yet, Toby.'

'But he must have told you when you can have time off?' he remarked impatiently.

Helen glanced nervously over her shoulder. 'Well, no ... but——'

'You can't be on duty twenty-four hours a day and not have time off. What the devil does the man think you are? A slave?'

'I don't really work all the time. In fact it doesn't feel as though I'm working at all,' she argued defensively, but Toby was not appeased.

'You have a life of your own to lead, Helen. Don't forget that.' There was a moment of absolute silence before he added: 'And you did promise to have dinner with me one evening.'

'Give me a little time, Toby,' she begged persuasively. 'I've only been here a little over a week, and I need time to settle in.'

'I suppose I shall just have to be patient,' he acknowleged grudgingly. 'What's your boss like?'

'Well . . .' She bit her lip and glanced over her shoulder once more. 'I don't see much of him.'

Toby was silent for a moment before he said understandingly, 'I suppose you can't really talk now.'

'Not really, no.'

'I think I ought to tell you that he isn't very popular among the villagers for closing his gates and not allowing them to use the short cut to the beach,' Toby continued confidentially. 'The Town Council has its usual red tape procedures to follow with regard to making the old path safe to use once more, and the villagers refuse to do anything about it themselves because they feel it's entirely up to the Council. It's a vicious circle, I'm afraid, and Simon Savage is at the centre of it.'

'It's not his fault that the powers that be allowed that path to become an accident hazard,' Helen jumped to her employer's defence. 'He actually had every right to close his gates to prevent his property from being used as a main thoroughfare.'

'The villagers don't think of it in that way,' Toby laughed.

'It's understandable,' Helen replied, cooling off considerably. 'Brock Castle has stood vacant more often than it's been occupied, and one can't blame them entirely if they began to regard it as public property.'

'You're right, of course,' Toby agreed amiably. 'You *will* let me know when you're free?'

'Yes, Toby, I will,' she replied, impatient now to end the conversation. 'And if you should see my aunt, give her my love and tell her not to worry.'

'I'll do that,' he sighed. 'Take care, Helen.'

She replaced the receiver, but the prickling sensation at the back of her neck made her glance over her shoulder to find Simon dwarfing the entrance to the living-room. Wondering frantically how much he had heard, and in no mood to cross swords with him, she murmured 'good afternoon' and headed towards the stairs on shaky legs.

'Just a minute,' his voice rapped out a command, and Helen paused on the second step and turned slowly to face him as he came towards her. 'I never intended listening in on your conversation, but I couldn't help overhearing part of it. I gather the village folk are still upset about the fact that I won't allow them through my property?'

'That's true,' she admitted, gripping the wooden balustrade to steady herself. His eyes were on a level with her own as he stood before her, and something in his glance warned her that he was not in the best of moods.

'I thought that their animosity would have been forgotten weeks ago,' he remonstrated harshly.

'Their animosity won't relax until they have a safe way of reaching the beach.'

'How they reach the damned beach is no concern of mine,' he insisted adamantly. 'The original path should never have been allowed to get into such a state of disrepair.'

'Mr Savage, despite the fact that I'm just as guilty of using the grounds of Brock Castle as a short cut to the beach, I admit that you were within your rights when you objected to your property being used in that way.' His dark eyes glittered strangely as she paused for breath, and she continued hastily, not wishing to probe too deeply. 'The point I wish to make is this. The authorities are taking longer than anticipated with the repairs, and there's no other route which can be used until they do.'

'Except the one through my grounds,' he concluded with a harsh twist to his lips.

Helen swallowed nervously and nodded, not daring to say more for fear of provoking the anger which appeared to be simmering beneath the surface of his self-control.

Lisa appeared on the landing and hurried down to Helen's side just as Simon turned on his heel and strode across the hall towards his study.

'Could we go and have another look at the baby doves this afternoon?' Lisa asked her with a nervous glance at her father's departing figure. 'They should be getting their feathers now.'

'Shall we go, then?' Helen suggested, expelling the air from her lungs as she followed Lisa, who appeared to be in an agitated hurry to reach their destination.

Her brief encounter with Lisa's father had disturbed Helen far more than she was prepared to admit. Despite his apparent unconcern, she knew intuitively that he was troubled by the result of his actions. He valued his privacy, and was entitled to it, but would he cling to his decision resolutely to the extent of endangering the safety of others?

'Why was Daddy so cross?' Lisa wanted to know when she had finally satisfied her desire to peep into the nest they had discovered on the first day after Helen's arrival.

'I don't think your daddy was angry about anything,' Helen prevaricated, emerging from her thoughts with a feeling of guilt. 'He's just a little worried about something.'

'What's he worried about?' Lisa asked suspiciously, her expression pinched and wary.

It was remarkable how swiftly the child's moods altered. One moment she would be comparatively relaxed, and the next she would be sullen and tense, Helen noticed as she sat down on the overturned tree stump and drew Lisa towards her.

'Lisa, your daddy's problems don't concern you, or me,' Helen replied, unobtrusively massaging the child's clenched fists until they lay relaxed in hers. 'Whatever your daddy's problems are, he'll sort them out himself.'

'Does he want to send me back to boarding school?'

'He's never mentioned anything to me about sending you to boarding school,' Helen assured her, somewhat startled.

Pink lips trembled pathetically. 'I don't want to go back to that awful boarding school, Helen. I want to stay with Daddy.'

Helen stared at her speechlessly for a moment before she gathered her close, and, on this occasion, Lisa appeared not to mind the embrace.

'Darling, I'm sure that if it's at all possible, your daddy would never send you away to school,' she reassured the child rashly. What did she know of how Simon Savage felt about the subject? He might consider boarding school as the only solution to his problem.

Lisa's arms slipped about Helen's neck. 'Will you tell Daddy not to send me away? Will you?'

Helen looked down into those large, pleading eyes, and a lump rose in her throat. 'I'll do my best, Lisa.'

CHAPTER FIVE

FACING Simon across the wide expanse of his desk that evening, Helen's carefully rehearsed speech disintegrated beneath his penetrating glance to leave her floundering helplessly.

'Was there anything else you wanted to tell me about Lisa's work?' he asked pertinently as she hovered on the edge of her chair.

'No—at least——' Furious with herself for allowing him to fluster her into stammering like an idiot, she said the first thing that came into her head. 'Lisa is afraid of being sent back to boarding school.'

There was a moment of absolute silence during which she could almost feel the shock waves of his anger. 'Did *you* mention the subject to her?'

'No,' she croaked, groaning inwardly as she clenched her hands in her lap. What on earth had possessed her to plunge into the subject so carelessly? 'She wanted to know why you looked so angry this afternoon, and I ...'

'Yes ... go on,' he prompted impatiently.

'I said that—that you were most probably worried about something.'

'Really? And then?'

'She announced, out of the blue, that she didn't want to be sent back to boarding school.' Her hands fluttered helplessly. 'I can only conclude that it's something which causes her more concern than you may realise.'

'What do you suggest I do about it?' he demanded with harsh cynicism. 'Go up to her and tell her that she can stop worrying about it, because I have no intention of sending her away to school eventually?'

'Would that be the truth?'

'No!' He thrust his chair back and rose to his feet with his hands clenched at his sides. 'The truth is, Miss Talbot, that I have no idea yet what I'm going to do with Lisa. I don't *want* to send her away, but I may *have* to.'

'Have you tried explaining this to her?' Helen asked as she watched him walk across to the hearth to stare broodingly into the fire.

'No, I haven't wanted to cause her any further unhappiness while the future was still so uncertain.'

'It might make all the difference to her to know that you have no intention of sending her away unless it becomes absolutely necessary,' she suggested tentatively, allowing her appreciative glance to dwell on the width of those forbidding shoulders turned towards her. 'She suffers from a feeling of insecurity, and I think this is basically her biggest problem.'

He turned to face her then, and she felt a quiver of anxiety race through her as he came towards her to perch on the edge of his desk with one muscular leg swinging to and fro in agitation.

'I gave up my home in the city for the peace and quiet Strafford had to offer, and because I thought the different surroundings might enhance her progress. What more can I do?'

'You could, perhaps, give her a little more of your time,' she challenged, but her heart lurched violently as he thrust his face towards her menacingly.

'Miss Talbot, I've been working day and night these past weeks to complete my latest work. The reason I've been doing this is so that Lisa and I could have more time together. All I need is a few more weeks,' he informed her with a mildness that did not deceive her. 'After that I shall be at her disposal whenever she wishes.'

Helen could find no fault with that, and admonished herself silently for practically accusing him of neglecting his daughter. 'I didn't realise...'

'No,' he interrupted mockingly. 'People seldom do, and I would thank you not to make snap judgements in future until you have all the facts straight.'

The shrill ring of the telephone extension on his desk pierced the silence, and, with a muttered exclamation, he stretched out an arm and lifted the receiver. Helen did not wait to listen in on the conversation, but made use of the opportunity to leave his study and return to her suite.

Her lounge was illuminated by the soft glow of the fire, and, not bothering to turn on the lights, she sat down in a chair and stared miserably at the carpet. Simon must think her an utter fool, she thought, cringing inwardly as she recalled the things she had said. She had wanted to discuss the matter with him in an effort to gain a better understanding of the child who had been placed in her care, but somehow the conversation had started all wrong, and the discussion had become a verbal sparring session.

She sighed as she switched on the small reading lamp and picked up a magazine, flicking idly through the pages, but too disturbed to take in the contents. Simon's face swam before her eyes, and his final rebuke still had the power to make her squirm. Why was it, she wondered irritably, that every time they met she was somehow on the defensive?

There was a light tap on her door, but it opened before she could raise herself, and Simon walked in, closing the door firmly behind him and leaning against it with his thumbs hooked into the broad leather belt about his hips. This was the first time since that day she had arrived that he had entered her rooms, and she knew intuitively that something had happened when she noticed his tight-lipped expression.

'I thought it might interest you to know what that telephone call was about,' he said tersely, and the frightened beat of her heart subsided slightly as he came close to the fire and stood staring down into it. "It was a Mr Bradley on the line. His little boy, Kenny, went down to the beach late this afternoon. He fell on the slippery path, received a severe crack on the head, and had to be rushed to the hospital in George. In between all the abusive language, I was able to gather that Mr Bradley will be sending his child's medical accounts to my address.'

'But that's absurd!'

'Tell Mr Bradley that,' he countered swiftly, turning to face her, and in the glow of the fire his scarred cheek gave him a cruel expression she was no longer sure he deserved.

'What are you going to do?'

'For one thing, I'm going to have a look at that damned path as soon as I get the opportunity,' he flung at her harshly, raking a hand through his dark hair.

'May I make a suggestion which might solve the problem?' Helen asked nervously, lowering her glance to the magazine still clutched in her hands, and when he made no effort to prevent her, she continued. 'There's a small gate in the side wall, beyond the servants' quarters, which could be opened to let the public through. You would still have your privacy, and the villagers would be appeased while they wait for something to be done about the safety of the original path.'

A dreadful silence followed her suggestion, and a frightened pulse throbbed painfully in her throat as she kept her eyes riveted to the expensive suede of his shoes, expecting at any moment to feel the irate lash of his tongue.

'Perhaps it's worth investigating.'

Her head shot up and she stared at him anxiously for a time as if to make sure that she had heard correctly, but the steady regard of his dark eyes held no mockery or cynicism, only an expression that was infinitely disturbing to her pulse rate.

'Could I offer you a cup of coffee?' she asked, longing

for something to do to relieve the tension as she rose to her feet and crossed the room to where a small table stood in the corner. 'It's instant, I'm afraid.'

'Thank you.'

'Bella very kindly supplied me with two cups and an electric kettle that wasn't in use,' she informed him eventually, glancing over her shoulder to discover that he had seated himself on the chair beside the one she had vacated. 'I hope you don't mind?'

'It seems that, in a matter of a little more than a week, you've managed to charm your way into the hearts of my staff,' he remarked with distinct mockery, and Helen stiffened instantly as she carried the tray towards their chairs and placed it on the small table he had drawn closer.

'If that's so, then it wasn't deliberate.'

'I wonder...' he said, his lips twitching slightly as he helped himself to a cup of coffee before observing her thoughtfully through narrowed eyes. 'You're doing remarkably well with Lisa, I notice. Do you intend to charm your way into my heart as well?'

Helen's slim body went taut with resentment. 'I don't know what you're talking about. I've never——'

'Oh, come now,' he interrupted harshly. 'I have yet to meet a woman, beautiful or otherwise, who doesn't make a practice of breaking as many hearts as she possibly can.'

'I don't intend to argue that point with you, Mr Savage, although it would appear as though you've met all the wrong women in your lifetime,' she said thickly, raising an involuntary hand to her throat where it felt as though she was being choked by her own heartbeat. 'I'm perfectly sure, though, that no woman will ever penetrate the armour you have so deliberately placed about your heart.'

What on earth was she doing, talking to him like this? she wondered frantically, but the next moment something happened to make her stare at him with barely concealed amazement. For the first time since she had met him, he threw back his head and laughed quite naturally and up-roariously. It was unbelievable the way it altered his expression; accentuating laughter lines about the eyes she had not noticed before, and relaxing the tautness about a mouth that seldom smiled without cynicism.

'You're quite right,' he said eventually, controlling himself, and she saw, with dismay, the harshness return to his features. 'I'm too well acquainted with the methods women employ to be fooled a second time.'

A *second time!* Had there been a first time? she wondered confusedly. There was apparently more to Simon's bitterness than she had imagined, and to allow her thoughts to run riot could only lead her to uncharitable conclusions, she decided sensibly, swinging the conversation to a safer topic.

'Mr Savage, if I want to drive into the village at times, may I have your permission to take Lisa with me?'

He placed his empty cup in the tray and took his time lighting a cigarette before he replied. 'I don't particularly wish to expose her to the public as yet.'

'Expose her to what public, for goodness' sake?' Helen blurted out in astonishment. 'No one in the village is going to pounce on the child for any reason, and it might do her the world of good to meet other people occasionally. She could make a few friends of her own age, and have them over to play in the afternoons.'

'No! I absolutely forbid it!'

'But why?'

'I can't afford to have children rushing through the house while I'm working, and——'

'But the grounds of Brock Castle are large enough to cope with a dozen children or more, without the necessity to disturb you in any way,' she interrupted argumentatively.

His lips twitched slightly. 'I was going to add that the reason for Lisa not attending school this year was that the doctors insisted that she was not to be excited in any way. Having children over to play might just do that.'

'Yes ... of course.' Helen bit her lip, angry with herself for not realising this before. 'I would still like her to meet my aunt. She's exceptionally good with children, and the children, incidentally, are very fond of her.'

Dark eyes, suspiciously mocking, pinned her to her chair as he eased his long, muscular limbs into a more comfortable position. 'What makes you think she might be good for Lisa?'

'I was in quite a state as a child when Aunt Ada took me into her home,' she replied, instantly regretting her remark as Simon sat waiting with obvious impatience for her to clarify her statement. It was not a subject she enjoyed discussing, but it was now vitally important to make this man realise that he could not keep his child a prisoner from the outside world. 'My father was a botanist, and his passion was yachting,' she explained abruptly. 'By combining those two ingredients, he developed a wanderlust that took him practically all over the world. My mother seldom allowed him to go on these excursions alone, and, on what was to be their last trip to the Peruvian jungle in South America, they were caught in a freak storm and reported lost at sea.'

Simon drew hard on his cigarette and frowned slightly. 'You were ... twelve when this happened?'

'Yes,' she nodded, surprised that he should have recalled this small detail which had arisen from her interview with him. 'I was a very frightened and bewildered twelve, I might add. I thought my world had come to an end until Aunt Ada took charge of me.'

It was a strange relief to have told him this, she realised during the ensuing silence, but his expression remained unfathomable as she waited for him to speak. She observed him surreptitiously as he flicked the remainder of his cigarette into the fire before rising to his feet, and she could not help but notice the way his faded denims clung tightly to muscular thighs. His shoulders moved in a careless gesture beneath his thick sweater, while strong fingers rubbed his jaw thoughtfully.

'If you think it might help Lisa to meet your aunt, then I have no objections,' he said at last, resuming his usual tight-lipped expression. 'But I don't want her unduly excited or upset in any way.'

Helen rose as well, and, for some reason, she could not think why, she placed her hand on his arm and felt the muscles go taut beneath her fingers. 'I promise to take good care of her, and ... thank you.'

He lowered his glance to her hand on his arm, and, embarrassed, she snatched it away. A brief smile lurked about his lips as he watched the colour rise in her cheeks, and she lowered her lashes to hide the confusion in her eyes.

'Thanks for the coffee, and goodnight ... Helen.'

He was gone before she could reply, but the sound of her name on his lips sent peculiar sensations chasing through her. 'Careful, Helen,' she warned herself severely. 'Simon Savage may have succeeded in placing protective armour about his heart, but yours is far too vulnerable and susceptible to escape unscathed if you don't do something about it quickly.'

While Lisa took her usual nap the following afternoon, Helen tidied the classroom, but the sound of the surf made her rush through her task to take that longed for stroll along the golden stretch of sand just beyond the grounds of Brock Castle.

It was an exceptionally warm day for midwinter, and Helen, in short-sleeved blouse and with her slacks rolled up to her knees, paddled through the shallow water as it pushed up on to the beach. She was alone on that strip of sand which was bordered by the sea on one side and dense bush on the other. This was how she had always preferred it since childhood; to be alone with her thoughts, to shed a tear perhaps, or to be at peace with herself and nature.

In the distance she could see the rugged cliffs of the mainland stretching out into the sea like a grasping arm with a lighthouse at its fingertips. Several seafaring vessels had come to grief, over the years, in the unpredictable currents along this coastline, but its picturesque beauty nevertheless enchanted the visitors who streamed yearly to the many holiday resorts further along the coast.

Helen raised her face into the breeze and drew the tangy air deep into her lungs, tasting the salty spray on her lips. It was an effervescent tonic to walk like this with the sound of the surf in her ears, and the warm sand curling away beneath her toes, but it was with a sense of ecstatic freedom that she stretched out her arms and did an impromptu dance on the sun-drenched beach.

Unaware that she was being observed, she continued to twirl about until, out of breath, she collapsed on to the sand and lay for some time staring at a lost little cloud making its arduous way across the clear blue sky. She closed her eyes eventually against the piercing rays of the sun, but the next moment a shadow fell across her, and her eyelids flew upwards to find the sky blotted out by muscular shoulders tanned a deep brown by the sun. Her frightened glance swept upwards from the broadness of a hair-roughened chest, and along the column of a strong throat, until it finally clashed with the hard face barely inches from her own.

There was no way she could make a dignified escape, for a strong arm had been planted firmly on either side of her, holding her captive, yet not touching her. She swallowed nervously as she looked up into those intensely dark eyes, and, to her astonishment, she noticed the peculiar golden flecks just round the pupuls. Strange that she had not noticed it before, she thought ridiculously as her glance slid over the jagged scar on his cheek, and she experienced the inexplicable longing to run the tips of her fingers along that raised line from temple to chin.

'There must be a reason for the exuberance you displayed a moment ago,' he mocked her, 'but I'm sure you could enlighten me.'

'Does there have to be a reason?' she questioned breathlessly, wishing he would move away so that she could get to her feet.

'There usually is,' he insisted, bending closer to observe the tiny pulse beating so rapidly against her throat. 'When a woman dances on the beach in the manner you've just done, then I can only conclude that it was for the benefit of some unsuspecting male.' His eyes glittered strangely, and Helen trembled at the onslaught his sheer maleness was making on her senses. 'Was it for my benefit, perhaps?'

Her breath locked in her throat. 'How dare you!'

'It wouldn't be the first time a woman has tried that method of attracting attention to herself,' he laughed mirthlessly, gripping her hand and drawing her roughly to her feet.

She dragged her hand free of his and brushed the sand from her hair and slacks as she stammered, 'I wouldn't— I've never—'

'But you just might,' he interrupted cynically. 'When the hunting instinct is strong enough, all women are the same.'

Helen paled visibly, her nails biting into her soft palms as she clenched her hands at her sides. 'You have a distorted opinion of women, Mr Savage.'

'Have I, Miss Talbot?'

It had been 'Helen' last night, she thought unhappily, suddenly intensely aware of the fact that he, too, was barefoot, and dressed only in a brief pair of shorts that hugged his slim hips and displayed to perfection his long muscular legs.

'Women aren't all as vile as you make them out to be,'

she said at last, aware that he had been waiting for her to reply.

'Then you admit that some are?'

'I admit nothing of the sort!'

'You're contradicting yourself, but it doesn't alter my opinion,' he said, his expression hardening. 'I've had excellent tutors on the subject, and all of them women. It's made me realise that there's not a woman on this earth whom one could trust or depend upon.'

He had turned away from her as he spoke, but the angry bitterness in his voice had not escaped her. Someone had hurt this man very deeply, she realised shakily. But who? And why?

Her gaze fastened on to a scar stretching from the centre of his chest across his ribs to his left side, but it did nothing to diminish the almost primitive aura of masculinity that surrounded him, making her aware of him in a way no other man had succeeded in doing before. Her glance slid upwards to his scarred cheek, and then she coloured with embarrassment as she realised that she had been caught staring.

His lips twisted sardonically. 'Do you find my scars distasteful?'

'N-no! They don't—bother me at all.'

Her stammering denial sounded anything but convincing, and she reprimanded herself silently when his eyes mirrored disbelief. How could she explain, without humiliating herself, the growing need she had to touch him, to run her fingers along his scars, and to feel the hard warmth of his body against her own?

'I've been considering that suggestion of yours,' his voice slashed cruelly through her thoughts.

Shaken to the very depth of her being that she should crave such intimacies with her employer, she echoed stupidly: 'Suggestion?'

His lips twisted slightly. 'To open up the side gate, remember?'

'Oh ... oh, yes,' she stammered, colouring profusely at the hint of amusement in his glance, and placing a hand against her ribs where her heart hammered heavily. 'Are you going to leave the gate open?'

'I think so, yes,' he nodded, and, at her look of surprise, he continued wryly. 'The problem is, how do I let everyone know of my decision? Do I walk through the village streets with a placard about my neck, stating, "The grounds of Brock Castle are now open to the public"?'

Realising instantly that he did not want to make an issue of the fact that he had finally relented, Helen said quickly, 'That won't be necessary. I'll drop a hint in the news-room, and it will spread like wildfire.'

'News-room?'

'My aunt's tea-room,' she explained with a brief laugh. 'Everyone goes there for a natter and a bit of scandal. Breathe a word, and it's blazed through the village in capital letters before you can bat an eyelid.'

Simon looked faintly relieved. 'Well, now that the problem of advertising is settled, I think I'll take a look at that old pathway everyone seems so concerned about.' He glanced down at her and raised a questioning eyebrow. 'Do you know the way?'

'Yes.'

'Come along, then.'

With Simon matching his long strides to hers, they made their way to where the path emerged among the tall red and yellow-wood trees which were festooned in moss, while arums and ferns grew wild in the moist undergrowth. Left undisturbed, it was a wild and enchanting paradise, but the overgrown, slippery path had already been the cause of one serious accident.

'Good God!' Helen heard Simon mutter beside her. 'Surely there must be some other way to reach the beach?'

'By road, yes. But for those who want to walk...' she paused significantly, casting a swift glance in his direction, but Simon had seen enough and gestured that they should return.

The walk back to Brock Castle was completed in silence, but once, when his arm had brushed against hers, she reacted violently, frightened out of her wits by the tingling sensation she was experiencing. Her reaction had not gone unnoticed, for his swift glance conveyed anger, and something else ... something that brought unwanted tears to her eyes. If Simon noticed, then he said nothing, but his stride quickened as if he was in a hurry to get away from her.

The tightness in Helen's chest did not diminish until she was safely in her suite, and only then did she release the tears she could find no explanation for.

At the first available opportunity Helen telephoned her aunt, asking her to drop a few statements in her tea-room to the effect that the side gate of Brock Castle would remain open in future for those who wished to make use of the grounds as a route to the beach.

'What on earth made him change his mind?' her aunt wanted to know. 'Was it Kenny Bradley's accident, perhaps?'

'I think Kenny's accident made him accept my suggestion more readily,' said Helen.

'*Your* suggestion!' the telephone almost exploded in her ear. 'You must have a certain amount of influence over him, then.'

'I have no influence at all really. It was merely a matter of making the right suggestion at the right time.'

'Well, whatever it was, good for you,' Aunt Ada laughed.

'You will remember to spread the word?' Helen asked anxiously.

'You can rely on me, my dear.'

Helen replaced the receiver with a feeling of satisfaction

before hurrying up to the classroom where Lisa was waiting for her.

As the lessons progressed that morning, Helen was once again made aware of the sensitivity of the child she was teaching. Lisa's handwriting was irregular, ranging from large and rounded to small, uneven letters. Thinking that it would help her if extra guide lines were drawn in her writing book, Helen picked up her ruler and approached Lisa. At once the child seemed to shrink in her desk, her eyes wide with fear.

'Lisa, what's the matter?' she asked anxiously, her heart twisting at the sight of that pale, quivering little face.

Lisa said nothing, but Helen followed her glance to the ruler in her own hand, and, as she drew her breath in sharply, an incredulous thought took shape in her mind.

'Did you think I was going to smack you?'

Lisa nodded, and then burst into a flood of tears.

Reacting instinctively, Helen lowered herself on to the small bench beside Lisa and clasped the shaking little body against her own.

'Lisa, I wasn't going to smack you,' she spoke soothingly, brushing the dark hair away from Lisa's damp cheeks, and slipping it behind a shell-like ear. 'What earthly reason is there for me to want to do something like that?'

'I—I thought you were going to s-smack me because my handwriting was bad,' Lisa explained jerkily through her sobs. 'Some of the o-others used to say they would.'

Understanding dawned like an electric light being flashed on in a darkened room, and Helen's arms tightened convulsively about Lisa.

'Darling,' she murmured, the endearment coming naturally from her lips. 'I'm sure they only said they would smack you in an effort to have your attention. They would never really have done so.'

'They were horrible,' Lisa cried, burying her face against Helen's breast. 'I *hated* them!'

'It's bad to hate others, Lisa,' Helen reprimanded gently, understanding her reasons, yet knowing that she should not approve.

'I can't help it,' Lisa replied with the honesty of a child. 'They made me hate them. They weren't like you—you're so different.'

Helen's heart warmed at the unexpected compliment, and she brushed her lips against the silky hair beneath her chin. 'I'm glad you think I'm different, Lisa, because I want you to believe me when I tell you that I'm here to help you in every way I can. Don't ever be afraid of me again, because I don't ever want to hurt you.'

Lisa raised her tear-stained face and, for the first time, there was no trace of suspicion in her wide, clear glance, only a tremulous smile of acceptance.

This incident had been an unexpected break-through that brought about a gradual change in their relationship during the days that followed. Lisa, like any other child, responded to the love and warmth Helen offered, opening up like a flower to expose what lay hidden within.

Nothing was mentioned when she reported to Simon's study each evening after dinner, but she was certain that he had become aware of the situation in some way, and that it pleased him.

After several weeks at Brock Castle, Lisa was no longer a stranger to Aunt Ada, for, after the first tentative visit, Lisa had been eager to go again.

'There's something I have to tell you,' Aunt Ada announced one afternoon when Helen and Lisa arrived at the tea-room. Lisa had gone through to the kitchen in search of her favourite cream doughnuts, and, despite the fact that there were no customers, Aunt Ada kept her voice lowered. 'Some very nasty remarks have been passed lately since you moved in at Brock Castle six weeks ago.'

Helen stiffened angrily. 'Have there?'

Ada Willis gestured impatiently. 'It won't do any good to

freeze me out, Helen. I did warn you that people would talk.'

'What are they saying?' Helen asked casually, but Aunt Ada's expression was enough to make her interrupt swiftly with, 'Perhaps it would be better if you *didn't* tell me!'

'Helen, I can't just sit back and allow people to speculate unkindly about you,' her aunt protested fiercely. 'There's a limit to my endurance.'

The temptingly familiar odour of freshly baked pastry filled Helen's nostrils and, for a moment, she was a child again, arriving from school and naturally ravenous at the sight of all the delicacies being prepared.

'My conscience is clear, Aunt Ada,' she said, dragging her thoughts back to the present, 'and it will remain so no matter what people say.'

'*I* believe you, and several others may,' Aunt Ada remarked adamantly, 'but there are those who'll continue to wonder.'

They were forced to discontinue their conversation when Lisa walked in, a half-eaten doughnut in her hand and a circle of cream about her mouth. She looked so comically satisfied with herself that Aunt Ada and Helen found it difficult not to laugh.

'This is my third doughnut,' Lisa announced proudly, taking another bite and adding a blob of cream to the tip of her nose in the process.

'Good heavens! Your father will skin me alive if you don't eat your dinner this evening,' Helen observed with a touch of humour as she grabbed a paper serviette from the nearest table and repaired some of the damage to Lisa's face.

'He won't really do that, will he?' Lisa asked with wide-eyed dismay.

'No,' Helen smiled reassuringly, inspecting Lisa's face. 'But he might just be very angry with me for allowing you to eat that many doughnuts so late in the afternoon, and he'll have reason to be angry if you don't eat your dinner, won't he?'

'I suppose so,' Lisa acknowledged, downcast.

Helen placed a finger beneath the small, pointed chin, and raised the child's face to hers. 'Let's hope that, just this once, your daddy will understand if you have no appetite at dinner, so eat up and let's go home.'

'If Daddy does get angry with you, you won't go away, will you?'

Helen stared at her for a moment, taking in the troubled expression in her eyes, and sensing the insecurity behind that question; an insecurity that had something to do with Lisa's small hand clutching so desperately at Helen's skirt.

'I won't go away, Lisa,' she reassured her, finding it difficult to speak with that peculiar tightness in her throat. 'Not even if your daddy is angry with me will I leave you.'

Satisfied, she ran out to where Helen's Mini was parked, and, her fears forgotten, climbed in and polished off the remainder of her doughnut.

Aunt Ada placed a hand on Helen's arm to detain her. 'That child needs you,' she said simply. 'To leave her now would be disastrous.'

Helen nodded silently. She had always known that she could depend on her aunt, but somehow her support at this moment was extremely gratifying.

'I must issue just one word of warning,' her aunt continued. 'Don't allow your tender heart to be enslaved by this child. The eventual parting is inevitable, and you'll only make it so much more difficult to endure.'

Aunt Ada's warning remained with Helen as she drove back to Brock Castle with Lisa, but there was a hollow feeling at the pit of her stomach that told her, in no uncertain terms, that the warning had come too late. She *was* enslaved, not only by this small child seated beside her, but by Simon Savage as well.

He was in her thoughts far too often for her own peace of

mind, his features coming between her and the task she was performing. But although she could forcibly eject him from her thoughts by day, she was entirely helpless at night when he invaded her dreams to mock her relentlessly. She would have to steel herself against this growing awareness, she told herself determinedly, or she might suffer a humilation far greater than she could ever imagine.

CHAPTER SIX

'MR Savage, is this really necessary?' Helen demanded one evening as she faltered in the middle of her usual daily report. 'Wouldn't it be more satisfactory if I gave you a monthly report on Lisa's progress?'

Simon turned from his usual stance beside the fire, and faced her with an enigmatic expression on his rugged face. 'You have a reason for suggesting this, I presume?'

As always, his glance was disconcerting, but she plunged into her explanation without hesitation. 'Lisa appears to have difficulty, at times, in concentrating on her work. I may succeed in holding her attention one day, but the next her mind may wander. The quality of her work fluctuates because of this, and I find myself giving you good and disturbingly bad reports almost alternately.'

'So you think a monthly report would be preferable?'

'It would make it so much easier for me to give you a general report over a specified period,' she insisted.

Simon observed her in silence for some time, his hands thrust firmly into the pockets of his pants, and a brooding expression in his dark eyes. It was difficult to guess at his thoughts, or to imagine his reaction, but the fact that he appeared to be considering her well-meant suggestion was enough to kindle a flicker of hope within her.

'Perhaps you're right,' he said at length.

'I know I am.'

'If we could all have such positive views on what's right or wrong, life might not be as complicated as it is,' he remarked with a touch of cynicism, gesturing expressively. 'All right, Miss Talbot, I have no objection to offer in this respect.'

'Thank you, but there is one other matter I'd like to discuss with you.' Helen hesitated briefly, a nervous fluttering at the pit of her stomach as she sensed a certain amount of agitation in his attitude. 'Would it be possible for you to acquire a record player for the classroom?'

'There's a record player in the living-room.'

'I know,' she nodded, thinking of the expensive equipment which he seldom used, 'but I would like to set aside some time each day for music appreciation, and we would only disturb you if we used the living-room for that.'

'Miss Talbot, I hired you to further my daughter's education, and not for the purpose of whiling away the time listening to pop records,' he said imperiously.

'That isn't my intention, Mr Savage, but it's nothing unusual these days to have a period, during school hours, just for listening to music, or children's stories. It's part of their education,' she explained with a pleading gesture.

'I don't agree with that.'

'You want her education to continue with as much normality as possible, don't you?'

'Yes, but I fail to see what the lack of—music appreciation—has to do with her education.'

'It has a tremendous amount to do with it, but if you don't want to buy a record player,' she pressed on hopefully, 'I could collect mine at my aunt's cottage for this purpose.'

'No!' His voice was like a whiplash, but he continued more civilly with, 'If a record player is such a necessity, then we can take a drive into the village tomorrow afternoon to see what the shops have to offer in a range suitable for the classroom.'

Helen stared at him for a moment in disbelief, but, afraid that he might retract his surprising offer, she murmured her thanks and decided to beat a hasty retreat.

'Helen . . .' She halted with her hand on the door-knob and turned slowly to find him standing beside his desk, an unlit cigarette between his agitated fingers. 'I would like you to know that I'm happy with the way you're handling Lisa, and I would like you to stay on, but ...'

'But?' she prompted, her wary glance shifting from the cigarette, which was in danger of being snapped in two, to the lines of bitterness etched so deeply on his face.

'You must be aware of the talk in the village?'

It was inevitable that the rumours would eventually reach him, she thought, sighing inwardly. 'Yes, I am, but I don't intend to lose any sleep over it.'

'I don't care about myself, Helen, but you don't deserve their nasty insinuations.'

His unexpected concern was surprising, and touching, but she was determined to remain firm about her initial decision. 'I knew what to expect when I accepted your offer of employment, and I have no intention of withdrawing now.'

'You may still regret adopting this attitude.'

'I can't leave Lisa now,' she argued desperately. 'She's only just beginning to trust me; to have confidence in me. To leave her now would be a criminal thing to do.'

A strange expression flitted across his face as he dropped the mutilated cigarette on to his desk and came towards her. Something in those dark, shadowy eyes meeting hers filled her with the curious sensation that she was being suspended over a chasm, and that this man before her held the lifeline in his strong, capable hands.

'If you feel so strongly about it, then I shan't mention the subject again, but if, at any time, you wish to change your mind ...'

'I shan't change my mind,' she said swiftly, intensely aware of his masculine appeal, and of the alarming effect his nearness was having on her pulse rate. His glance softened momentarily before he resumed his tight-lipped expression and stepped away from her.

'Goodnight, Helen.'

His dismissal had been like the shutters being drawn after allowing her a brief glimpse at something elusive, she thought as she made her way slowly up to her suite. Was it possible that she could have imagined that subtle change of expression, simply because it was what she so desperately longed to see?

She opened the door to her lounge and went inside. Bella had lit the fire in the hearth, and Helen stood for a moment staring down into the flames, aware of a wild longing stirring within her; a longing that had to be suppressed at all costs if she wished to remain at Brock Castle. For some inexplicable reason Simon Savage had the power to disturb her emotionally in a way no other man had ever succeeded. She feared him, and yet...

'You're an idiot, Helen Talbot!' she told herself angrily, thrusting her thoughts away from her as she went through to Lisa's room to make sure that she was settled comfortably.

As promised, Simon brought his car round to the front after lunch, for the trip into the village, and Helen's eyes widened perceptibly as she came down the stone steps with Lisa's hand in hers. The gleaming silver Bentley, with its exquisitely plush interior, was the most beautiful thing she had ever seen, and it was so absolutely right for a man like Simon Savage.

'I had it shipped out from England a few months ago,' he answered her unspoken query.

'It's beautiful,' she acknowledged as he helped Lisa into the back seat.

Seated beside him, eventually, she soon forgot her nervousness as she relaxed in the comfort of the well-sprung seat, and stole surreptitious glances at those strong, well-shaped hands on the steering wheel. Just as with everything else, he was in complete control, and she had little doubt that, if he should ever remarry, he would control his wife in

8 Harlequin Romances for only $1⁰⁰

PLUS!
"Harlequin" FREE

Featuring a *complete* Harlequin novel . . .
plus romantic short stories, an author's
own story, travel, crafts, cooking and
dozens of other special features!

see inside . . .

Take these **8** Harlequin Romances for only $**1**⁰⁰

In a villa above the eternal city of Rome . . . in a fashionable London apartment . . .

The Clouded Veil
by Isobel Chace

Elinor had been virtually a widow for two years, her husband Zachary having disappeared somewhere in Morocco. Now, out of the blue, he had turned up again — but he now seemed like a stranger to her. Could they possibly manage to save their marriage?

Hold Me Captive
by Margaret Pargeter

After a serious family quarrel, Amanda felt the need to get away quickly. But her flight led to great difficulties when she found herself in the middle of Dartmoor with a disconcerting stranger named Jason Meade. Out of the frying pan and . . .?

Beyond The Foothills
by Essie Summers

After unwelcome publicity, Marilla St. John retreated to the country for a while. But she was not prepared for the encounter with Rufus Sinclair, a confirmed bachelor who had heard that Marilla was a husband-hunter. How could she convince him he was wrong?

Flight Into Yesterday
by Margaret Way

To Lang Frazer, Natalie was just a spoiled, heartless girl who revelled in hurting her father and her stepmother, Britt. But Natalie saw Britt as the woman who had ruined her relationship with her father. And what business was it of Lang's anyway?

in a tense room of a small town hospital . . . this is Harlequin's world of romance!

Rainbow For Megan
by Jane Corrier

Megan had always looked on Alain as an older brother, so it was embarrassing for both of them when people began to link their names romantically. To prove everyone wrong, Megan went to her good-looking boss for assistance — but only succeeded in complicating matters!

Summer Rainfall
by Kerry Allyne

A twenty-acre farm in New South Wales wasn't a very large legacy, but it meant a lot to Kim, and she was determined to go and live there. She was certainly not going to sell the place to the local big landowner — however attractive he might be!

The Emerald Garden
by Katrina Britt

A bitter family quarrel had kept Vinney apart from her mother and her sister, Denise. But now they were all together, and Vinney was hoping for a happier relationship at last. But then she fell in love with the man Denise was going to marry . . .

Château D'Armor
by Rebecca Stratton

Jesamine's assignment, doing research into an old French family in a romantic chateau, promised to be fascinating. But her work, and her relationship with the attractive Paul D'Armor led her into deeper waters than she had expected . . .

Here's a wonderful opportunity to enjoy the excitement of romantic adventure at its best! We publish over *eighty million* romances a year so we *know* the kind of stories you want! These are some of the most moving romantic novels ever written . . . each one a spellbinding classic of the struggles, conflicts and tenderness of love! These are the books you can't put down! That's why we can afford to make this generous introductory offer, to get you started on what we hope will be a long and beautiful relationship with Harlequin Romances!

PRINTED IN CANADA

**Business
Reply Mail**

No Postage Stamp
Necessary if Mailed
in Canada

Postage will be paid by

Harlequin Reader Service

649 Ontario St.,
Stratford, Ontario
N5A 6W2

Canada Post
Postes
Canada
021

PRINTED IN CANADA

exactly the same way, bending her to his will whenever the need arose.

Startled by her thoughts, she glanced at him swiftly, but his attention was on the road ahead, his face an inscrutable mask. For a moment her glance lingered on the strong line of his jaw, then she turned her head away, experiencing that familiar rush of warmth that quickened her pulse.

If the villagers were speculating about her presence at Brock Castle, then they were tactful enough not to show their feelings at the sight of Helen in the company of her employer and his daughter, while the shop assistants were clearly overawed by Simon's imposing presence. The record player was bought without much fuss, and while Simon did the necessary transactions, Helen and Lisa went out to the car to wait for him.

'Helen!' Her arm was taken in a firm grip as she helped Lisa into the Bentley, and she was swung round to face Dr Toby Warren, his strong features clearly displaying his delight at this unexpected meeting. 'I've been waiting for that promised telephone call, and I'd almost given up hope of ever seeing you again.'

A wave of guilt swept over Helen. She had almost completely forgotten about Toby Warren, and the promise she had given to dine with him one evening.

'I'm sorry, Toby, but I've been rather busy,' she smiled apologetically. 'And so have you, I believe, what with a minor gastro epidemic in the village.'

She was intensely aware of the fact that Lisa was observing them with wide-eyed curiosity, and that Simon would join them at any moment, but Toby seemed unaware of her growing anxiety as he glanced into the car and exchanged a few words with Lisa.

He straightened eventually, his glance persuasive. 'The epidemic is over now and, if you're not too busy, what about having dinner with me this evening?'

'I'd love to, Toby, but I——'

Helen stopped in mid-sentence as she saw Simon emerge from the shop, an angry frown between his eyes as he approached them. Toby followed the direction of her gaze, and his lips tightened perceptibly.

'Good afternoon, Dr Warren,' Simon greeted him coolly. 'I gather you know Miss Talbot?'

'Yes, Helen and I are old friends,' Toby remarked casually, ignoring Helen's surprised glance at his deliberate attempt to give a false impression. 'I've invited her out to dinner with me this evening, if that's in order with you?'

Helen held her breath as the two men faced each other, Simon, tall and dark, with his scarred face an impenetrable mask, and Toby, almost a head shorter, displaying a practised calmness so common to men of his profession.

The tension in the atmosphere was finally relieved when Simon remarked coldly, 'Miss Talbot doesn't need my permission to have dinner with you, Dr Warren. I dare say she's old enough to make up her own mind in that respect.'

'That's settled, then,' Toby replied swiftly, in an obvious hurry to be on his way. 'I'll pick you up at six, Helen.'

'Toby, I don't think——' she began protestingly, but, with a wave of his hand, he was gone, and she found herself facing Simon with a feeling of helpless embarrassment.

'It appears that your mind has been made up for you,' he mocked harshly as he opened the door for her. 'Women are always such undecided creatures.'

She threw back her head and glanced up at him, but she bit back a sharp reply at the controlled anger in his manner, and climbed into the car.

The journey back to Brock Castle was completed in an uncomfortable silence. The relaxed atmosphere had disintegrated from the moment Toby had put in an appearance, Helen thought as she stared miserably ahead of her and tried to ignore the flicker of pain that stirred within her.

'Can we play some of these records this afternoon,

Helen?' Lisa asked as Jacob came hurrying down the steps towards them.

'Who gave you permission to call Miss Talbot by her name?' Simon demanded instantly.

Lisa appeared to shrink against the back seat, and Helen intervened swiftly, 'I gave her permission, Mr Savage.'

He allowed the matter to pass for the moment as he swung his legs out of the car and walked round to the boot, and Helen smiled encouragingly at Lisa as they followed his example.

It was not until Jacob hurried inside with his burden that Simon faced Helen once more. 'Well, seeing that things are nice and friendly between the two of you, perhaps you'd better call me Simon.'

'I—I couldn't do that,' she stammered breathlessly.

'Why not?' he demanded with raised eyebrows. 'If I may use your name, then why can't you use mine?'

'That's different,' she argued, avoiding his glance. 'You're my employer.'

'And if, as your employer, I insist?'

'It ... would be better if you didn't.'

'Helen?' Lisa tugged impatiently at her hand, and the tension lessened considerably.

'Go up to your room, Lisa. Helen ...' Simon hesitated significantly, 'will be up later.' Lisa's face clouded, but she did as she was told and hurried inside, leaving Helen alone with Simon, and with her growing sense of alarm as his hand touched her elbow. 'I would like to see you for a moment—privately.'

He did not release her until they reached the seclusion of his study, and even then, as they sat facing each other across his desk, she could still feel the pressure of his strong fingers just above her elbow.

'I've never expected you to literally tie yourself to Lisa,' he said without preamble, 'and I didn't care very much for Dr Warren's attitude. Neither did I like the veiled suggestion that I kept you a prisoner here at Brock Castle.'

Helen understood suddenly the reason for his anger, and tried to smooth it over as best she could. 'The whole thing is entirely my own fault. He asked me to have dinner with him some time ago, and it slipped my mind completely, but I don't think that Dr Warren actually intended to imply that I was being kept a prisoner. That's just ridiculous, and I've never considered myself as such, anyway.'

'Then please take whatever free time you need, within reason, as long as I'm kept informed, and arrangements have been made with Bella to keep an eye on Lisa.' His lips twisted cynically. 'I don't wish to break up your affair with Dr Warren.'

The colour surged into Helen's cheeks, and then receded to leave her deathly pale. 'I am not having an *affair* with Dr Warren!'

'Very well, then. I don't wish to cause a rift in your ... friendship,' he supplemented mockingly, extracting a key from the drawer and dropping it on to the desk within her reach. 'Here's a spare key for the front door if you should come in late.'

After a moment of complete inertia, she took the cold piece of steel between her fingers. 'Thank you.'

'You may go,' he said abruptly, rising to his feet, and she stared at him for a moment with a bewildered expression in her eyes before she rose stiffly and left the room.

Why, whenever he dismissed her in that abrupt manner, did she always have that peculiar feeling that he had slammed a door in her face? she wondered distractedly as she made her way up the stairs in search of Lisa.

The evening spent with Toby was not entirely the success he might have hoped for. Helen's thoughts were constantly with Lisa, and the fear that something might happen in her absence which would cause Simon's wrath to erupt over her head.

Toby was, however, a pleasant companion; uncomplicated and easy to talk to. But this, too, made her think of Simon, and the difficulty in communicating with him without being angered, or on the defensive. His remarks nearly always had a sting to them, as if the very fact that she was a woman annoyed him.

'I don't wish to bring up the subject of Simon Savage and his daughter,' Toby interrupted her thoughts as they lingered over coffee, 'but I would like to know how Lisa is progressing, from a physical point of view.'

It was inevitable that Toby should eventually mention the subject which had kept her thoughts occupied most of the evening, she realised guiltily. 'There's been an improvement lately,' she said.

His grey eyes smiled mischievously. 'You realise, of course, that you've outlasted all your predecessors?'

'So I gather.'

'What's the secret of your success?'

'I don't know whether I *am* such a success,' she replied thoughtfully, allowing her glance to dwell briefly on the couple holding hands at the table beside their own. 'Lisa is still very subdued. She never speaks of her mother, her brother, or the accident, but she broods about it. I'm almost certain that, if I could get her to talk about them, she would be a different child.'

'Have you ever thought of trying shock tactics?'

'No . . .' She frowned slightly. 'Do you think it wise?'

'I'm not a psychiatrist, but I should think it's worth trying,' Toby replied seriously, glancing over his shoulder at the couples swaying together on the dance floor. 'Come on, let's dance.'

He took her hand and led her on to the floor, holding her a little closer than was absolutely necessary as they danced in tune to the music.

'You're very lovely, Helen,' he whispered somewhere

above her ear when the band finally played a slow waltz. 'Too lovely to bury yourself behind the walls of Brock Castle.'

She coloured slightly at the compliment. 'I enjoy my job, Toby, and it's very rewarding.'

'I don't want to talk about your job,' he laughed softly. 'I want to talk about *you*.'

'I thought you wanted to dance,' she teased lightly, and, with a rueful smile, Toby obliged.

They drifted back into a lighthearted conversation, steering away from subjects that could become involved and personal. But as he parked his car beneath the shadows of Brock Castle's turrets, later that evening, and switched off the lights, Toby turned towards her with quiet determination.

'I must see more of you, Helen. Will you let me take you for a drive into the country one afternoon? We could stop somewhere for tea, and just enjoy the scenery.'

'I . . . don't know.' Her uneasy glance went swiftly to the light just barely visible behind the living-room curtains, almost as if she expected at any moment to see them swept aside to reveal her employer's disapproving figure.

Toby's arm slid along the backrest behind her as he leaned closer persuasively. 'I won't take no for an answer.'

'All right, Toby,' she agreed quickly, opening the door and stepping quickly from the car as she sensed his intention.

'Helen——'

'Goodnight, Toby,' she interrupted gently, 'and thank you for a lovely evening.'

She had closed the car door and was hurrying up the steps before he could prevent her. She heard him start the car as she reached the front door, and, turning, she saw him wave briefly before he disappeared down the drive.

Moments later she stood inside the darkened hallway, the living-room light illuminating her way towards the stairs, but her heart skipped a beat as a tall shadow fell across the floor and halted her progress.

'Helen.' She turned to find Simon standing in the doorway, tall and faintly menacing, his features dark and shadowy. 'May I see you in my study for a moment, please?'

The hall clock told her that it was past eleven as he stood aside for her to enter before him. Her nervousness increased when he finally closed the study door behind him and came purposefully towards her, but he merely gestured that she should remove her coat and take a seat beside the fire.

His glance swept down the length of her, taking in the colourful silk of her gown where it clung to her figure. 'Did you have a pleasant evening?'

She glanced at him suspiciously, but there was no sign of mockery in his expression as he faced her. 'It was very pleasant, thank you, Mr Savage.'

'Simon,' he corrected, walking towards the cabinet in the corner. 'I was going to pour myself a drink before going to bed. Could I offer you something? A light wine perhaps?'

'Thank you.' She felt slightly puzzled by his behaviour, and unable to understand this sudden amiability he was displaying towards her, but she tried to relax as he returned to the fireside with a glass in each hand. The seconds ticked by as they sat sipping their drinks, and still Simon made no effort to speak. Finally, the suspense too much for her, she was forced to interrupt his brooding silence. 'Was there something you wished to discuss with me?'

He stared at her blankly for a moment before his brow cleared. 'I shall be driving to Cape Town tomorrow on business. I should have told you earlier, but it slipped my mind.'

'Oh . . .' Her heart sank like a piece of lead. 'Will you be away long?'

'A week at the most,' he announced, draining his glass.

'You'll have the staff close at hand, so you'll be quite safe.'

'I'm sure I shall be.'

'There is just one thing I must insist on,' he continued firmly. 'I don't want you to go out at night while I'm away.'

'I would never dream of leaving Lisa alone at night,' she assured him quickly, and slightly annoyed that he could think she would contemplate such an action.

'You will be seeing Dr Warren again, I take it?'

His question was disconcerting, but she met his penetrating glance unwaveringly. 'Yes, I think so.'

Her body tensed as she waited for him to pass some remark to mock her association with Toby, but, to her surprise, he merely rose to his feet and stood with his back to the fire, his hands thrust into the pockets of his slacks.

'Don't hesitate to call Dr Warren if you feel Lisa needs medical attention, and if you should want to contact me urgently for some reason while I'm away, I've written down my telephone number, also that of Godfrey Muller, on the notepad beside the telephone.'

'Godfrey Muller . . . the producer?' she asked in surprise, recognising the name.

'Yes,' his lips tightened slightly. 'Do you know him?'

'No . . . but anyone with an interest in the theatre has heard of Godfrey Muller,' she explained, running a nervous finger along the rim of her glass as she avoided the intensity of his glance.

'Do you have an interest in the theatre?'

'Purely as an observer, yes.'

'Have you ever considered the possibility of a stage career?'

'Good heavens, no,' she laughed with a touch of embarrassment. 'We once did *Hamlet* at school, and I was a dreadful Ophelia!' His mood was strange, she thought as she glanced at him covertly, and, if she could trust her intuition, she could almost believe that he was depressed. 'Have you finished your play?'

He registered a certain amount of surprise before he gestured towards the neatly tied manuscript on his desk. 'I completed it this evening.'

'Aren't you happy with it?' she probed carefully.

'It's a good play . . .' he paused significantly, a flicker of a smile about his mouth, '. . . if you're prepared to look at life without those infernal rose-tinted glasses. I've spat out all my venom on to those pages, and it leaves me with a hollowness inside which generally lasts a day or two before I start building up a new supply for the next play.' If he noticed her shocked expression, then he decided to overlook it as he gestured towards her glass. 'More wine?'

'No, thank you. It's late——'

'And I've kept you longer than I'd intended,' Simon finished for her, walking across to where she had placed her coat over the arm of a chair.

Helen picked up her evening bag and rose to her feet. She *was* tired, and slightly lightheaded after that glass of wine, she thought as he draped her camelhair coat about her. Could she also blame the wine for the strange weakness in her knees at the lingering pressure of his hands against her shoulders?

'I shall be leaving early tomorrow morning, so say goodbye to Lisa for me,' he said, his voice an unconscious caress that did strange things to her heart. She closed her eyes for a moment, savouring forbidden sensations as he drew her back against the hardness of his chest. For one brief moment his breath was warm against her temple, then he pushed her firmly towards the door. 'Goodnight, Helen.'

She left the study without looking back; not daring to for fear of encountering his mockery. A wave of shame engulfed her when she realised that, if he had not placed her so firmly from him, she would have been quite content to remain there resting against him. It was perhaps just as well that he would be away for a few days. It would give her time to overcome her embarrassment, and to renew her grip on her seemingly wayward emotions.

With Simon's absence, something vital was missing from Brock Castle. Except for the evening meal, which they shared together, Helen seldom saw him, but his presence in the house was enough to give each day new meaning. It was ridiculous, and inexplicable, but she had no intention of delving too deeply beneath the surface of her emotions. Despite his scars, he was not a man one could easily ignore, or forget, and this was something which was causing her a considerable amount of concern. In a few months' time she would have to walk out of his life, and she would prefer it to be accomplished with a minimum of fuss, and without any personal involvement. A little stab of pain mocked her at this thought, but she chose to ignore it.

Lisa entered her bedroom one morning while she was brushing her hair, and the child's fascinated glance lingered on the small ivory box in the opened drawer.

'Will you make it play again?' she asked, timidly touching the carved lid, and, completely oblivious of the fact that she had given herself away, she glanced up at Helen expectantly.

Helen turned the key at the back of the box, and recalled that first afternoon at Brock Castle when she had hoped to entice Lisa into her room with the sound of the intriguing Eastern music. Now, as the tinkling melody filled the room, she observed Lisa closely, and noticed the total absorption with which she was listening until it had wound down completely.

'Make it play again, please, Helen?' Lisa begged and, laughingly, Helen obliged.

'What about going for a long walk on the beach this morning?' she suggested eventually when the musical box had wound itself down for the third time.

'Could we?' Lisa asked eagerly, her eyes alight as she

thought of something. 'Would you show me your special cave this morning?'

'My special——' Helen stopped, then laughed suddenly as she recalled how she had endeavoured to gain Lisa's interest by mentioning the cave she had discovered as a child. 'Of course I'll take you to my special cave if you'd like me to.'

Lisa's expression became almost excited, and there was an eagerness in her manner when they finally made their way along the beach to where the mainland began its sharp rise into a cliff face. Wild grass and leafy bushes grew in the sandy soil below it, and Helen made her way directly to where a large rock jutted out like an overhanging roof amidst the others. With a piece of driftwood she brushed aside the branches of a thorn bush, exposing the entrance to a small cave, which was actually not very much more than a cavity, hollowed out by the sea when the tide was full.

'Could we go inside?' Lisa asked eagerly, edging towards the opening.

'I suppose we could,' Helen replied, 'but it doesn't go in very far.'

She took Lisa's hand as they entered, but it had been many years since she had paid a visit to this cave, and she was unprepared for the sudden lowering of the roof which her adult height could not accommodate. She gasped as she felt the sharp blow against her forehead and clutched at the side wall. There was a blinding flash of light before the pain set in, and then she began to shake with reaction.

'I don't like it in here,' she heard Lisa say in a quivering voice. 'It's cold, and it smells funny.'

It had been a mistake to bring Lisa, in her nervous and over-imaginative state, to this old and musty-smelling cave, Helen realised as the pain subsided to a dull throb. Simon would be angered, too, if he discovered they had played truant from the classroom that morning for an escapade as silly as this.

Without a word, she took Lisa's hand and they retraced their steps, exchanging the damp smell of the cave for the fresh air outside.

'You're bleeding!' Lisa cried, her eyes wide with fright as she stared up at Helen.

Helen raised her hand swiftly to her head, and was surprised to notice the bloodstains on her fingertips. Murmuring reassurance to Lisa, she quickly dabbed at the wound with her handkerchief. 'Don't upset yourself, darling. It's probably just a scratch, but let's go home so I can take a proper look at it.'

With Lisa clutching her hand anxiously, she made her way back to Brock Castle as quickly as she could, but Helen felt decidedly shaky and faint when she finally inspected the damage in her bathroom mirror. There was an ugly gash just below her hairline on the right side of her forehead and, after cleaning away most of the congealed blood, she came to the inexpert opinion that she would most probably need to have it treated medically.

'It's my fault,' Lisa sobbed. 'I asked you to take me to the cave.'

With an improvised dressing covering the wound, Helen glanced ruefully at her blood-spattered blouse, but she ignored it for the moment as she sat down on the rim of the bath and drew Lisa towards her.

'It wasn't your fault at all, Lisa. I should have remembered that I'm much taller now than the last time I entered the cave.'

'But——'

'No buts,' Helen smiled, wiping away Lisa's tears. 'It was my own stupid fault, and no one else's. Now, let's go and see if we can find Dr Warren at his surgery, shall we?'

'Will he have to put stitches in just as they did with Daddy?'

Yes, she had forgotten—Lisa must still have vivid memories of the accident they had been involved in, and she was more than angry with herself now for having brought these memories back so sharply.

'I don't think it's as serious as that, but Dr Warren will know what to do.'

Helen was wrong, however, for Toby had to cut away a little of her hair to stitch the wound. Her eyes were smarting by the time he had finished, but she smiled at Lisa and saw the anxiety replaced by a look of relief.

'Does it feel better now?' Lisa asked tremulously.

'*Much* better.'

'It might not feel so good tomorrow,' Toby warned, rinsing his hands in the wash basin. 'There's a considerable amount of swelling, and it's likely to become discoloured.'

'How kind of you to warn me that I shall look even more of a fright tomorrow,' Helen teased.

Toby turned and laughed slightly as he came towards her, touching her cheek with cool fingers. 'You could never look a fright, Helen.'

She lowered her glance swiftly beneath the intensity of his gaze, and slid off the stool. 'Thank you very much, Toby. I think it's time we returned to Brock Castle before someone discovers we're missing.'

'The stitches can be removed in a week's time, and if you have any pain, take those tablets I gave you,' he said, gesturing towards the small envelope in her hand as he accompanied them out to her car. 'And don't forget that I'm coming to take you out for a drive one afternoon.'

'I won't forget, Toby,' she promised, helping Lisa into the car and sliding into the driver's seat of her blue Mini. 'And thank you again.'

The days passed slowly, and uneventfully, after that unfortunate incident, but on their next excursion ino the village they paid a visit to Aunt Ada.

'Good heavens, what happened to you?' her aunt demanded as she glimpsed the strip of adhesive on Helen's forehead.

'A slight accident,' Helen explained quickly, not wishing to dwell on the subject for Lisa's sake. 'I walked into a wall.'

'In the cave,' Lisa supplied gravely.

'The cave?' Aunt Ada echoed incredulously.

'We went ex-ex——'

'Exploring,' Helen filled in for her, smothering a smile as she glanced from Lisa's innocent little face into her aunt's confused grey eyes.

It was at that moment that a spaniel puppy was brought into her aunt's tea-room on a leash, and Lisa, shedding her serious manner for the first time to become an ordinary dewy-eyed child, rushed towards the wriggling bundle of fur to fondle and fuss it.

'I wish I had a puppy like this one,' Lisa whispered as she went down on her knees beside it, and Helen's glance met her aunt's with complete understanding.

Ada Willis enticed Lisa into the kitchen, tempting her with freshly baked doughnuts, while Helen questioned the woman with the puppy. Mrs Bradley, the mother of the little boy who had injured himself on the slippery path to the beach, had a spaniel who had given birth to a litter of eight. There were still five left, the woman told Helen.

Leaving Lisa in Aunt Ada's care, Helen drove swiftly to Mrs Bradley's home, and a few minutes later she had selected a puppy similar to the one Lisa had fussed over with such ecstasy.

'How much do I owe you, Mrs Bradley?' Helen asked, opening her handbag and extracting her purse.

'Is the puppy for Lisa Savage?'

'Yes,' Helen replied, instantly on her guard as she expected the woman to cancel the sale out of pique.

'You can have it,' Mrs Bradley announced, looking slightly uncomfortable. 'After the way Mr Savage paid all Kenny's hospital expenses I couldn't possibly take money from you.'

Helen stared at her for a moment, unable to explain the emotions that surged through her. 'I . . . didn't know.'

'My husband said some terrible things to Mr Savage at the time, but he regretted it afterwards,' Mrs Bradley explained shamefacedly. 'We thought no more about it after he telephoned Mr Savage again and apologised, that's why it came as a complete surprise to us when the hospital told us that the account had been paid.'

There was, after all, a spark of humanity in Simon Savage, Helen thought happily when she eventually drove back to the tea-room with the puppy on the back seat, investigating the basket she had bought it to sleep in.

'I've something for you in the car,' she told Lisa some minutes later.

'What is it?'

'It's a surprise.' Helen took her hand. 'Come and have a look.'

Lisa walked beside her obediently, but she showed no real interest in this unexpected gift until Helen opened the door and revealed the excited puppy on the back seat of her Mini.

'It's a puppy!' Lisa exclaimed excitedly as she clambered into the back and scooped it into her arms. 'Aunty Ada, come and see what I've got!'

Aunt Ada, who had followed them outside, peered into the car. 'It looks like a real little scamp to me.'

'That's what his name must be—Scampy,' Lisa announced, cuddling the golden-haired pup with excitement and disbelief mingling in her large eyes. 'Is it mine? Is he really mine, Helen?'

'He's yours, if you want him,' Helen smiled.

'Oh, yes. Yes, I *do* want him,' Lisa nodded firmly. 'And you want to stay with me too, don't you, Scampy.'

For an answer the pup wriggled in her arms in an effort to lick her face, and Lisa's happy laughter made the two women smile at each other as they recalled a similar situation several years ago with a pup called 'Spats'.

'Well, it's time we went home,' Helen announced, dropping a light kiss on her aunt's cheek. 'Cheerio, Aunt Ada, and thanks for keeping an eye on Lisa.'

She slipped behind the wheel and, with a last wave, pulled away from the kerb, but Lisa was quite oblivious of everything except her new-found friend.

'Do you think Daddy will let me keep him?'

'I don't see why not,' Helen answered, somewhat surprised. The thought had never occurred to her that Simon might object to his daughter having a dog to play with, but it was too late now to consider such a possibility. 'There's plenty of space for it to run about at Brock Castle without getting under anyone's feet.'

'Can he sleep in my room with me?'

'Just for tonight, perhaps,' Helen relented, turning off into the lane towards Brock Castle.

The remainder of the afternoon was spent on the spacious lawn with Lisa and Scampy, and Helen was amazed at the transformation in the child. Serious, often sullen, and seldom displaying more than a slight smile, Lisa's laughter, as she rolled on the grass with Scampy, did something to Helen that brought a constant rush of tears to her eyes.

'You're crying,' Lisa remarked once when she came close enough to notice, and Helen laughed tremulously as she hugged her.

'Perhaps it's because I'm so happy to know that you're happy too.'

If Lisa was puzzled by her reply, then it did not last long, for Scampy claimed her attention once more and she raced round the lawn with the pup in hot pursuit.

Scampy, his tummy full and exhausted by the unaccustomed exercise that afternoon, lay curled up in his basket that evening when Helen tucked Lisa up for the night.

'Helen,' Lisa murmured sleepily, holding out her arms.

'Thank you for giving me such a lovely present.'

Lisa's arms were wound tightly about Helen's neck, and her heart ached with love for this child. Within a matter of a few weeks, Lisa had wormed her way into her affections, capturing her heart in a way that made her aware of a growing anxiety for the day that she would have to leave.

'God bless, Lisa,' she whispered as she tucked her in, then she turned out the light and left the room, lest Lisa should see the tears that hovered on her lashes.

It had been a happy day; a day of surprises and new beginnings. Perhaps, soon, she would discover the reason for Lisa's odd behaviour at times, and the brooding thoughts behind her sad eyes. But, until then, she would have to be patient and tactful in her efforts to unravel the fears which resulted so often in nightmares.

It did not take much ingenuity on her part to realise that Simon's marriage had not been a happy one. His wife's name was never mentioned; not by him, nor by Lisa, and the accident that had killed his wife and son was a subject no one seemed eager to talk about. The entire incident was shrouded in a veil of mystery that intrigued Helen. Was it merely the loss of his loved ones that made him so bitter, or was there more to it than most people surmised? And why, whenever Lisa thrashed about on her bed during a nightmare, did she cry out, begging not to be given a hiding and swearing that not a word would pass her lips?

Helen sighed and passed a tired hand over her eyes. She had exhausted every possible theory on the subject, but she was no nearer the truth than she had been on that first night when Lisa's screams had awakened her. And although Lisa's nightmares occurred less frequently now, the reason for them still lurked beneath the surface of her conscious mind.

It was perhaps her duty to discuss this matter with Simon, but she knew intuitively that the problem was of a personal nature, and that he would not relish the fact that she, a stranger, should pry into his affairs, no matter how valid the reason.

Simon ... a harsh, twisted and embittered man. Would she ever understand him? Would he ever allow anyone close enough to know the man behind the mask?

CHAPTER SEVEN

THE Saturday morning had begun in its usual happy mood. There were no lessons to keep them indoors, and they were going down to the beach to romp on the sand, or just to sit and watch the ships passing in the distance. Scampy made a mischievous third that day, barking at seagulls, chasing after imaginary objects, and generally making a nuisance of himself as he kicked up sand.

It was a warm day and Helen, dressed in an old blouse and faded denims, had removed her scarf from about her neck to fasten Lisa's hair into a pony-tail, as she had done with her own before leaving the house. Except for a few anglers on the rocks further along the beach, they were alone, and Scampy, ears flapping and tail wagging, promptly stampeded their newly-built sand castles to the ground. At first, Lisa appeared to be angered by this, then it became a game which continued until their thirst finally drove them home.

That was when everything suddenly went wrong. Scampy dashed through the kitchen, down the passage, and into the hallway, with Lisa a close second, and Helen, breathless and laughing, dashing after them.

It was innocent fun, but the situation was all at once chaotic. Simon had returned unexpectedly while they had been out, and he stood observing their approach with an elegantly dressed woman at his side. Helen's laughter died in her throat as she came to a jerky stop, while Scampy ran mad circles round the two astonished people, with Lisa dashing wildly after him. It was Simon who finally caught the pup by the back of the neck, lifting it to hang helplessly from his hand, while his guest gripped Lisa's arm and drew her roughly to a standstill.

'What is the meaning of this?' Simon demanded coldly, holding Scampy up for inspection. 'And who does this item belong to?'

'He's mine,' Lisa owned without hesitation as she disengaged herself from the woman's grip, and stepped towards her father. 'Helen gave him to me.'

Two pairs of eyes were suddenly trained on Helen where she stood rooted to the floor, Simon's angry and accusing, while his companion's registered surprise and speculative curiosity as they took in every detail of Helen's dishevelled appearance in comparison with her own immaculate attire.

'And who is this?' the woman asked disdainfully.

Simon placed Scampy unceremoniously into Lisa's arms and ordered her outside before he straightened. 'This,' he gestured towards Helen, his face a mask of suppressed fury, 'is Lisa's governess, Helen Talbot. Helen, this is Lisa's aunt, Rosalind Allen.'

So this was Brenda Allen's sister, Helen thought as she admired her stylish emerald green suit while murmuring something appropriate. She shifted her weight uncomfortably from one foot to the other as Rosalind Allen inclined her dark head slightly, her green glance appraising Helen coolly, and then dismissing her as unimportant.

'A bit young, isn't she?' Rosalind remarked, turning to face Simon, and Helen experienced a flicker of anger at being treated as though she did not exist.

'Oh, I don't know,' Simon remarked with forced casualness as he unbuttoned the jacket of his grey suit, and thrust his hands into the pockets of his pants. His eyes swept Helen from head to foot until her cheeks were stained a delicate pink. 'She may be young, but she's had some excellent results with Lisa.'

Helen lowered her lashes to hide her pleasure at this

unexpected compliment, but she was certain that his anger had in no way diminished.

'An older woman would have been more satisfactory, I would have thought.'

'Older women aren't that easy to find,' Simon smiled slightly. 'And time was running out.'

'I hope you know what you're doing,' Rosalind sighed. 'Oh, well, I think I'll go up to my room for a while.'

'Do that, Rosalind,' Simon agreed, and with a last disparaging glance at Helen, Rosalind mounted the stairs. Then Simon's dark eyes appraised Helen once more. 'I would like a private word with you, Miss Talbot.'

She was "Miss Talbot" again, Helen thought unhappily, her heartbeat quickening nervously as Simon jerked his head in the direction of the study. It was a silent command she found frightening as she brushed past him and went ahead.

He closed the study door behind him and leaned against it for a moment, his arms folded across his chest. 'I don't recall my permission being asked for Lisa to have a dog?'

'No, I'm sorry, but . . .' She bit her lip and wished that she did not feel so much like a child about to be severely reprimanded.

'But what?'

'You don't object, surely?'

'I object most strongly,' he said with a harshness that made her take an involuntary step backwards as he approached her. 'Just after we moved in here she wanted me to get her a dog, and I made it quite clear to her that it was out of the question.' His glance sharpened. 'Didn't she tell you this?'

'Yes.' Helen crossed her fingers behind her back as she lied in her effort to protect Lisa.

'I suppose you thought that I was being unnecessarily harsh on her?' he demanded, the lividness of the scar on his cheek telling her clearly of his anger.

'Not harsh,' she contradicted softly, 'but a little un-reasonable, perhaps?'

His eyes narrowed perceptibly. 'It never occurred to you, did it, that I might have refused because of our inevitable return to the city? What do you think we're going to do with a dog in a flat?'

It *was* a thought which had never occurred to her, and she felt chilled by it. Simon was right—a flat was no place to keep a dog in, and her foolish gift had now created a problem which might never have existed.

'I'm sorry,' she whispered with remorse as she brushed past him on her way to the door. 'I'll explain the situation to Lisa and take the pup back to where it came from.'

'Helen.' His fingers closed about her arm, their warmth arousing tingling sensations that were not unpleasant, as he drew her towards the window and pointed to where Lisa sat beneath the oak tree with Scampy cradled lovingly in her arms. 'I'll work out some way of accommodating that pup. You can't take it from her now.'

'I know, but——' She caught her trembling lip between her teeth, but there was nothing she could do about the tears that shimmered in her eyes.

'I'm not as callous as you would like to believe,' he mocked her, his nearness a sweet agony she knew she had to escape from. 'Do you think I don't appreciate what that animal could mean to her?'

'I know you're not as callous as you *pretend* to be,' she replied, recovering herself swiftly and blinking away her tears.

'Do I sense an undercurrent of something in that re-mark?'

He was suddenly much too close for comfort. The warm smell of him, and the lingering aroma of his particular brand of shaving cream attacked her senses in the most devastating way. She moved away from him slightly to ease the tension within her, and idly fingered the bronzed replica of an eagle in flight which stood on his desk.

'I managed to get that pup from Kenny Bradley's mother.'

'So?' he remarked, lighting a cigarette and observing her with narrowed eyes through a haze of smoke.

'She told me you'd paid Kenny's hospital bill.'

'And now you think you've found a chink in my armour?'

His expression was granite-hard as he stood there beside the window, his one hand thrust into his pocket, and the other bringing a cigarette to his lips. His attitude did not invite a reply from her, but she nevertheless heard herself saying: 'A very little one, perhaps.'

'Be careful, Helen,' he warned with derisive mockery in his eyes, 'or you may find me very human when it comes to the fundamental things in life.'

She had trespassed on to forbidden territory, and she had to get out fast. 'Is Miss Allen staying long?'

His smouldering eyes registered momentary blankness before he raised his heavy eyebrows in surprise. 'Two or three days. She seldom stays longer. Why?'

'I just wondered,' she replied calmly, recalling the way Lisa had practically ignored her aunt. 'Does Lisa get on well with her?'

'No.' Helen raised her glance sharply, and surprised an odd little smile on his lips as he continued. 'Rosalind hasn't your natural instinct where children are concerned. She does her best, but...'

He left his sentence unfinished and Helen blushed slightly. This was the second time he had complimented her in some way since that unfortunate incident in the hallway.

'I—I'd better go out to Lisa,' she stammered, heading towards the door and very nearly tripping on the carpet in her confusion.

'Helen . . .' It was odd how the sound of her name on his lips always sent a shiver of pleasure through her. 'Thank you.'

'What for?' she asked in surprise as she swung round to face him.

'For your kindness to Lisa.'

He was not looking at her as he put out his cigarette in the silver ashtray on his desk, and her glance lingered on his dark head with the hint of greyness in the sideburns on his cheek. 'I happen to be very fond of her.'

'I'm sure that the feeling is mutual as far as Lisa is concerned.'

'I would like to think so,' she admitted softly, wanting to escape while her legs were still willing to carry her firmly from his presence, but he turned then and captured her glance.

'There's something different about your hair,' he remarked, and she felt almost faint when his hand brushed aside the hair she had combed so carefully to conceal the strip of adhesive. Then, as his glance darkened, something stilled within her. 'How did this happen?'

'I'm afraid that, at my suggestion, we played truant one morning and went exploring in an old cave. I miscalculated the height of the roof,' she confessed truthfully.

'How badly did you hurt yourself?'

His fingers touched the strip of adhesive, and lingered in her hair, making coherent thought almost impossible as she stammered, 'It n-needed a f-few stitches.'

'My God,' he whispered. 'I ought to lecture you severely, but I dare say you'll think twice before playing truant a second time.'

She nodded wordlessly, relieved that he had decided to overlook their misdemeanour on this occasion, and then, as he turned away abruptly, she made her escape, choking back a rush of tears she could not afford to release at that moment.

Lisa was scowling when Helen found her in the garden. 'I know what *she*'s doing here again.'

She could only be Rosalind Allen, Helen thought frowningly as she sat down beside Lisa on the grass and allowed Scampy to clamber all over her in a welcoming gesture. 'It's only natural that your aunt would want to see you occasionally.'

'She doesn't come here to see me,' Lisa announced, her scowl deepening. 'She comes here to get money from Daddy.'

'Lisa!'

'It's true! I heard her!'

'You ... heard her?' Helen questioned on a breathless note, not at all sure that she should allow Lisa to continue.

'Yes,' Lisa nodded, gathering Scampy into her arms and clutching him against her as if he were a child. 'She told Daddy that if he didn't give her money, she would go to the police and tell them about something terrible Daddy had done.'

It felt to Helen as if a giant hand had squeezed the breath from her lungs. Was this possible? Or was it a figment of Lisa's imagination? She could have listened in on a conversation, and misunderstood, for children are at times inclined to place their own interpretation on adult discussions. But what if Lisa had spoken the truth? Was it possible that Rosalind Allen was blackmailing Simon for some obscure reason? She shook her head slightly to clear her mind of these staggering thoughts.

'Lisa, you must never tell anyone else what you've just told me,' she warned with deep concern. 'Do you promise?'

Lisa shook her head vigorously. 'I *haven't* told anyone else. Only you.'

'Then let's keep it a secret between us, shall we?' Helen suggested with relief, jumping up and holding out her hand. 'Come on, I'm dying for a cold drink, and Scampy must be thirsty too.'

It took a tremendous effort to rid her mind of the statement Lisa had made, for the questions kept returning to haunt her. It couldn't be true, she kept telling herself. It *had* to be a misunderstanding. But, when they sat down to dinner that evening, the questions rotated agonisingly through her mind, making her wish that she could tear them physically from her brain.

Rosalind made a notable effort to converse with Lisa, but the child stared sullenly at her plate and answered in monosyllables. It was perhaps impolite of Lisa to show so clearly that she disliked her aunt, but Helen had a strong suspicion that Rosalind was, in some way, deliberately provoking the child in an effort to prove something to Simon, for she glanced at him continually when her attempts failed, and the look in her eyes could only be interpreted as triumphant.

The muscles tightened in Simon's jaw, and Helen realised that, if she wanted to avoid a nasty scene, this was the moment to step into the breach. She rose swiftly to her feet and, standing beside Lisa's chair, she met Simon's furious glance calmly.

'It's been a long day for Lisa, and she's tired. Do I have your permission to take her up to her room?'

Simon appeared to be struggling with several emotions before he, too, rose to his feet and nodded. 'Goodnight, Lisa, and say goodnight to your aunt Rosalind.'

Helen could feel the slight body tense beneath her hand, but she steered her gently in the direction of the woman who sat observing them with narrowed eyes. Lisa was clever enough to know just how far she could go and, raising her cheek obediently for her aunt's kiss, she said "goodnight" politely, and returned to Helen's side.

'Perhaps we could spend some time together tomorrow when you're not so tired,' Rosalind suggested adroitly, and Helen felt Lisa's fingers grip hers tightly.

'Perhaps,' Lisa echoed dully, but as they mounted the

stairs she turned to Helen, and said anxiously, 'I don't want
to be alone with her, Helen.'

There was a nervous twitching about her lips, and Helen
silently cursed Rosalind Allen for putting in an appearance
at a time when Lisa was on the brink of overcoming her
unnatural fears.

'If you don't want to see her alone, my poppet, then you
shan't. And that's a promise,' Helen said firmly, and Lisa's
tense expression relaxed gradually.

Some time later, with Scampy settled in his basket in a
corner of the laundry, and with Lisa tucked up in bed,
Helen found her thoughts returning to the alarming possibility that Simon was being blackmailed. There *had* to be
some reasonable explanation for Lisa's statement, but how
would she ever discover the truth without being accused of
interference?

Her thoughts were running in chaotic circles when she
eventually decided to have a bath and call it a day, physically and mentally. The whole thing was beyond her, and the
more she thought about it, the more confused she became.

It was long past eleven that evening when she gave up
the struggle to sleep, and slipped out of bed. What she
needed was fresh air, she decided, putting on her coat over
her nightdress, and fastening the buttons. She peeped into
Lisa's room to make sure that she was asleep, then she
opened her door quietly and made her way down the
passage to the door that opened up into the tower.

Her slippered feet were silent on the stone steps leading
upwards, and in the dim light her shadow cast weird patterns against the wall. She was not afraid, she had been up
there once before when sleep had evaded her, and had
found the silence and solitude comforting companions until
her eyelids drooped with fatigue. She negotiated the final
bend in the stairs and opened the heavy door. The cool sea
air rushed to meet her, and she drew it deep into her lungs
as she leaned against the low wall. The moon was full, its

soft glow changing the sea into a silvery carpet that shimmered in the night.

That was how her parents must have seen it on so many occasions during their frequent trips across the oceans. How many times had they perhaps sat on deck at night, when the sea was calm and the moon was full, just listening to the gentle lapping of the waves against the hull of their yacht? Did they also experience that strange feeling that they were at peace with the world, and that no one, and nothing, could touch them?

The stars were clustered together in a clear sky, so close, in fact, that she could delude herself into thinking that she need only reach out to pluck one. Just one, perhaps, to give to Simon as a token of ... her love? No! Never! But a million stars witnessed her surrender to the blinding truth.

Why Simon? she asked herself. Why a man who no longer had a place in his life for women? A man so embittered by life that there was no room in his heart for love? Why could it not have been someone like Toby? He was gentle, kind, and more than half in love with her, so why did she have to fall in love with a man like Simon?

A slight scraping sound behind her made her turn sharply, and her breath locked in her throat as the object of her thoughts approached her, his hands dug deep into the pockets of his thick dressing-gown.

'Couldn't you sleep?'

'No,' she croaked, the wild beat of her heart thundering in her ears at the sight of him.

'Neither could I,' he admitted, leaning against the parapet and glancing up at the sky. 'I come here often at night when I need to think.'

His face was harsh in the moonlight, the lines from nose to mouth lending a touch of cruelty to lips that must have known tender moments of passion ... once. A futile longing made her turn away from him with a hand against her heart as it continued its painful, erratic beat.

'I think I'll go in now,' she forced the words past her unwilling lips.

'Do you find my company distasteful?'

'No, of *course* not!' the words were ripped from her heart.

'Then stay,' he commanded quietly, and she returned to her place beside the parapet, a comfortable distance from him. 'It's remarkable how brilliant the stars are at this time of night,' he continued unperturbed. 'Do you know that one hardly ever notices the stars in the city? I know *I* never have.'

'Perhaps it's because life is so rushed in the city that we never stop for a moment to enjoy the peace and beauty of nature.'

Was that her voice replying so calmly to his statement? she wondered as he turned towards her.

'If you could choose, would you live in the city, or would you prefer somewhere picturesque and quiet like Strafford?'

It was a strange question, but she replied truthfully, 'I would choose somewhere quiet.'

'And if you should marry a man some day whose profession took him to the city?'

'Then I would go with him, naturally.'

He regarded her closely for a moment before he asked: 'You wouldn't object?'

'I would never stand in his way. Besides...' She bit her lip nervously, wondering at the purpose of this discussion, and where it would eventually lead.

'Yes?' he prompted, lessening the gap between them and awakening a frightened pulse at the base of her throat.

'When you ... l-love someone, your happiness lies with that person, no m-matter where you live.'

Her faltering, but sincere statement, changed his face into a mask of ruthless cynicism. 'That's a very noble attitude to adopt, but, once you have the noose around some poor devil's neck, you'll forget these pretty words you've just uttered, and he'll have to do what *you* dictate.'

'Simon, I'm not like that. I love you!' her heart cried, but she said instead: 'If he does, then he's a weakling and deserves no better.'

'And if he doesn't, he spends the rest of his life fighting for his ideals, and his very existence.'

She was up against a wall, and he was thrusting a sword into a heart that was throbbing with a love that was tender and new.

'You make marriage sound like a battlefield,' she whispered, fighting against the despair in her heart.

'That's just what it is,' he continued relentlessly. 'A battlefield where a man has to pit his wits against the devious tactics women employ.'

'Marriage isn't like that at all, and neither are women as devious as you imply.'

'Aren't they?'

'You *know* they're not.'

He moved then, and Helen backed away against the wall, feeling it dig into her ribs just above the waist. Simon imprisoned her by placing a hand on either side of her against the parapet, and she was helplessly trapped. His breath stirred her hair, and her pulse quickened alarmingly. She was in a vulnerable position, and he had deliberately placed her there, by the trend of his conversation.

'You're no different from other women, Helen,' he accused, her nearness awakening emotions she had tried so valiantly to suppress. 'If I were to take you in my arms now, you would be soft and pliable, but underneath you're a scheming temptress just like the rest of them.'

'That's not true!'

His hands were against her back, strong and compelling as they drew her against the hardness of his body. The roughness of his dressing-gown was beneath her palms as she endeavoured to push him away, but a paralysing weakness drove the strength from her limbs.

'You're trembling,' he mocked her, and, as she was about to deny this, her head was forced back by the pressure of his mouth against her own.

His kiss was ruthless and demanding, at first, then it became deliberately sensual, brushing her lips apart to awaken her to sensations never before experienced. She knew that she had to resist, but it was a futile thought while every nerve tingled in response to his touch. She felt his hand fumble with the top button of her coat, then his lips found the warm softness of her slender throat, and, finally, the gentle hollow where a tiny pulse throbbed in response. It was madness to allow him to make love to her like this when it could only lead to heartache ... and, with this sobering thought, she began to struggle against him.

'Don't!' she moaned softly into the stillness of the night, which had, until that moment, only been disturbed by the heavy beat of her heart.

'Your lips say "don't", but your body says "yes",' he mocked as he released her abruptly. 'That proves my point that all women are false.'

Helen recovered swiftly, drawing air into her lungs along a throat that ached. 'What did you expect me to do? Did you think I would allow you to make love to me just so that you could say that, like all women, I was using my body to trap you?'

'You're not going to tell me that the thought didn't occur to you?'

That was the final, and most fatal, thrust of the sword, and she fled from him with a choked cry, down the spiral steps, along the short passage, and through her lounge to her bedroom.

How could he? she asked herself, shaking uncontrollably as she sank down on to her bed and covered her hot face with trembling hands. How dare he trample on her emotions as if they were less than dust beneath his feet! How dare he imply that she would give her kisses lightly in an effort to trap him!

Her anger at that moment overshadowed the pain, and she clung to it, like someone clinging to a raft in stormy seas, until sleep claimed her some minutes later.

Helen kept out of Simon's way the Sunday morning, but it was inevitable that they should meet for lunch with a guest in the house. Her determination to wipe out the memory of what had happened between them, and Simon's coldly detached attitude, saved her a considerable amount of embarrassment. He gave her the coolest of glances, and then completely ignored her as he entered into a lengthy theatrical discussion with Rosalind, which he knew very well Helen was not capable of contributing to.

That afternoon, as she did most afternoons, Helen sat in the classroom making preparations for the following day's lessons. It came as a surprise, therefore, when there was a knock at the door and Rosalind entered, bringing with her a waft of expensive perfume. Helen could not imagine that she was at all interested in Lisa's work, for her attitude was faintly bored when Helen replied to her questions. This was not the reason for her unprecedented visit, Helen thought wryly as she pulled out a chair and invited Rosalind to sit down. The reason was more likely her own presence at Brock Castle as Lisa's governess. Rosalind wasted no time either in coming to the point.

'How long have you been in Simon's employ?'

Green eyes, curiously brilliant beneath dark lashes, regarded Helen closely as she replied, 'Just over two months.'

'And you'll be staying until Lisa is well enough to return to boarding school?—as she undoubtedly will, if I have anything to do with it.'

If Rosalind Allen had anything to do with it, Helen could not help thinking, then Lisa would seldom see the inside of her father's home, but she said: 'If Mr Savage finds me satisfactory, yes.'

'I'm sure he does,' Rosalind remarked, an unpleasant smile curving her attractive lips. 'He never *could* resist a pretty face and figure.'

'My appearance has nothing to do with my work,' Helen replied distastefully, but the remark had filled her with a slight uneasiness.

'Don't you think so?' the husky voice was tinged with sarcasm. 'Are you in love with him?'

Shaken considerably, Helen somehow managed to maintain a measure of outward calmness. 'Miss Allen, I fail to see the reason for these personal questions.'

Rosalind brushed aside her protestation in the manner of a woman who was used to having her own way. 'Don't dodge the issue, Miss ... er ... Talbot. Are you in love with him?'

Their glances clashed and Helen threw caution aside as she said tritely, 'If I am then it's none of your business.'

'Oh, but it is, my dear,' Rosalind replied with a smile of satisfaction that chilled Helen. 'You see, Simon won't be marrying anyone but myself, because—if he doesn't I could make life very uncomfortable for him.'

Fear licked at Helen's heart. 'In what way?'

'My dear, he tried to poison my sister on one occasion, and if I hadn't been in the house at the time to rush her to the hospital, she would have died. I also heard him threaten to kill her just an hour or so before the accident.' She stopped, allowing her statement to take the desired effect before she continued. 'Just a few words in the right direction could ruin Simon if the case had to be reopened, and these facts had to be brought out into the open.'

Was this perhaps what Lisa had overheard? Helen wondered distractedly. Was there, after all, some truth in Lisa's innocent statement that Simon was paying Rosalind to keep her quiet? It was a horrifying thought she preferred not to dwell on, and one she found rather difficult to believe.

'You can't blackmail someone into marriage, and then expect to find happiness,' she protested eventually when she had managed to gather her wits about her.

'You must have realised, Miss Talbot, that Simon is a very wealthy man, and that's the only ingredient I need to make me happy,' Rosalind replied complacently. 'And who could be a better stepmother to Lisa than her mother's sister?'

'You must excuse me, Miss Allen, but I have work to do,' Helen said stiffly as a wave of disgust swept over her, but Rosalind took the knowledge that she was being dismissed quite calmly as she rose to her feet.

'Just keep in mind the fact that he's *mine*, Miss Talbot. You wouldn't want to see Simon's name slandered in the newspapers, would you?' she asked in a tone that was clearly threatening.

Helen rose as well, feeling slightly sick at the thought that someone as lovely as Rosalind Allen could be so twisted and corrupt inside.

'I think I'm beginning to understand many things now which have puzzled me in the past, and I'm grateful to you, Miss Allen.'

A faint hint of perfume in the air was all that remained as a physical reminder of her visitor, and Helen slumped back into her chair, burying her face in her hands. What she had told Rosalind was the truth. She was beginning to understand why Simon had such a low opinion of women, if Rosalind was anything to judge by when it came to the women he had known. Was it possible that Brenda Allen, with her beauty and sensitivity on stage, could have resembled her sister in character, as well as looks? Helen shuddered at the thought.

Helen did not believe for one moment that Simon had deliberately tried to poison his wife, and neither would he have staged an accident by which his own life, and that of his children, could have been endangered. He was always in such complete control of his emotions, that he would never be foolish enough to kill someone in anger, or otherwise, and this she knew with a certainty she could not explain.

Having come to this conclusion, she stared at the papers before her, but a more frightening question arose in her mind as if printed in capital letters. If Simon had not committed such a dastardly crime, then what had he done that he should pay out sums of money for Rosalind's silence? And would he eventually pay the ultimate price by entering into a loveless marriage with this woman who had not the slightest concern for his happiness?

Helen's timid fantasy, that she might eventually show Simon the meaning of true happiness, died a violent death before it was even born. She might have been able to temper his harshness, or to penetrate his defences, but she could not fight the hold this woman had over him without knowing the complete truth, and Simon would *never* take her into his confidence. She was an employee; someone he could bombard verbally with his theories, or amuse himself with, if he so wished, but he would never consider her worthy of sharing his problems.

She groaned as the knife twisted in her heart, making her oblivious of everything except the pain that swept through her. Loving Simon was an agony she had never known before. She had loved Richard in a quiet sort of way, and she had wanted to marry him very much, but her feelings for him had been nothing compared to this overwhelming longing and desire that possessed her. Every nerve in her body appeared to be sensitively alert to the sound of Simon's voice, his step, and his mere presence under the same roof with her. She had been a fool to allow this to happen, and yet she had never been more vibrantly alive; more aware of herself as a woman.

She had no idea how long she had remained there in the classroom, engrossed in her thoughts and oblivious of her surroundings, and she jumped violently when the door was opened without the customary knock.

'Aren't you coming to have tea?' Lisa asked with a hint of her father's authority in her voice.

After all her improbable, and highly illogical, thoughts and dreams, Lisa's query was too mundane not to be humorous, Helen thought as she pushed back her chair and laughed shakily. She could not blame Lisa if she found her behaviour strange, for what child would understand the sometimes pathetic hopes and dreams of an adult, or the reason for slightly hysterical humour when an important subject such as tea was mentioned?

CHAPTER EIGHT

ROSALIND returned to Cape Town after the weekend, and
as time went by Helen became accustomed to her now
frequent visits to Brock Castle, and she very much suspected that Rosalind was now more determined than ever to
get Simon into her clutches. She had also become accustomed to Lisa's odd behaviour when her aunt was in the
house, for it was as if, for some reason, she feared Rosalind,
and had sensed some unpleasantness beneath the surface of
her aunt's charming exterior.

During this time Helen avoided being alone with Simon
as much as possible, and her efforts were simplified by the
fact that he often journeyed to Cape Town, and remained
several days. The production of his play had begun, and,
from the little she could gather, Simon always took a
personal interest in this side of things.

Helen saw more of Toby Warren than ever before as the
weeks passed, and his relaxing company was a welcome
change from Simon's austere presence. Toby often took
Lisa and herself for a drive into the country when Simon
was away, or met them on the beach when the weather was
warm, joining them for tea afterwards at the house before
leaving on his rounds. She valued his friendship, although
she more than suspected that his feelings went further than
that. Common sense told her to break off their relationship,
yet, when she was with him, she did not have the heart to
hurt him, and hoped that her attitude would convey clearly
that she had nothing more than friendship to give.

The poplar trees were casting long shadows across the
lawn, late one afternoon in October, when Simon's silver

Bentley came up the drive. They had not expected him until the following day, and Lisa behaved most surprisingly by jumping up and running to meet him, with Scampy, now a little more than a pup, beating her to it. Helen stood frozen as Simon climbed out of his car and stood watching Lisa's approach. There was a chilling hesitation as she reached him, then he swung her up in his arms and hugged her briefly before lowering her to the ground.

Helen approached more slowly, swallowing at the lump in her throat as she fought against the tears that stung her eyelids. The barriers were down between father and daughter, and Helen's joy was indescribable. She was also very aware of his dark glance, taking in her cool silk blouse and pleated skirt, as she stepped on to the gravel path where he and Lisa stood waiting.

'Are you as happy as Lisa to see me back?'

Her heart somersaulted uncomfortably. 'I hope you had a pleasant journey, Mr Savage.'

His eyes mocked her deliberate evasion, and he bowed slightly. 'Very pleasant, thank you, Helen.'

They entered the house with Lisa between them, and Bella appeared miraculously with a tray of coffee which she carried into the living-room. Helen poured, and then Lisa took the floor, relating to Simon everything they had done in his absence, and, innocently, not omitting the fact that they had spent a considerable amount of time with Toby. Simon listened with surprising tolerance, his glance meeting Helen's only briefly at the mention of Toby's name, but it was enough to send the colour rushing to her cheeks. She knew what he must be thinking, but there was no way of disproving his theory without making herself look an idiot.

'I noticed that the side gate has been closed,' he remarked when Lisa paused for breath.

'An official from the Council telephoned while you were away,' she told him quietly. 'The old pathway has now been cleared, and there's no longer any need for the villagers to make use of your property. He asked me to thank you for your kindness, and that you would be receiving an official letter to this effect. There was no need for the gate to remain open after that, so I asked Jacob to put on the padlock.'

'I see.'

It was difficult to tell from his expression whether he was pleased to receive this news, or whether he had become so accustomed to the idea of everyone trooping through his property that their absence would be almost a loss.

After dinner that evening, when she was free, she went for her usual stroll on the beach. She had not gone far when she realised that she was being followed, and that the lean, muscular figure coming towards her across the sand was unmistakably Simon. Her heart leapt into her throat, and she succumbed to a wild desire to run. It was a ridiculous thing to do, and futile, for his long legs closed the gap between them with ease, and her flying pace was halted when his fingers bit into the soft flesh of her arm and jerked her about. She stood for a moment, catching her breath, and wishing desperately that she could crawl under the nearest bush in an effort to escape.

'Stop trying to avoid me, Helen,' he said eventually, releasing her arm, and the night air was cool against her skin where his warm hand had been a moment ago.

'I'm not avoiding you.'

'Yes, you are,' he insisted, his voice deep and harsh, but infinitely pleasing. 'Whenever I come near you these days, you run like a frightened rabbit.'

She turned away from his disturbing presence, and stared out across the sea where the moon had risen to perform its own special magic. 'It's pointless indulging in a discussion with you, because we always end up arguing.'

'We argue because you won't accept the truth.'

She shook her head. 'I can't accept your distorted ideas.'

'That's because you prefer to walk about with your eyes

closed, weaving a world of fantasy about yourself, and so
avoiding the truth,' he persisted.

'Oh, what's the use?'

Her hands fluttered in a helpless gesture, then his fingers
gripped her shoulders, turning her to face him. His touch
was unbearably sweet, his nearness a pleasurable agony and,
with the moon playing gently across his scarred cheek, she
loved him with a desperate longing to place her head against
the comforting breadth of his chest, and to feel once again
the strength of his arms about her.

She could never explain afterwards whether it had been
the effect of the moon, or whether she had somehow relayed
her thoughts to him, but there had been no desire to
struggle for release when his lips found hers, and drew from
them a response that made his arms tighten about her
slender waist until she felt certain that her ribs were in
danger of cracking.

'Simon,' she whispered brokenly as his lips trailed across
her cheek and found a vulnerable spot behind her ear.

'I thought you were never going to use my name,' he
murmured against her throat before his lips brushed hers
apart, and created such pleasurable sensations that she
trembled in his arms.

'What do you want of me, Simon?' she begged, her
hands finding delight in the muscles rippling against his
shoulders.

'I did warn you that I was only human, remember?' he
remarked with a touch of cynicism as his hand slipped
beneath her blouse and moved warm and caressingly
against her skin. 'You're a very desirable woman, Helen,
and you're not a child. Do I have to spell it out for you?'

Her hands stilled against his shoulders, and a coldness
crept beneath her skin as she drew away from him, placing
some distance between them. 'No ... no, you don't have to
spell it out. I understand perfectly.'

'And?'

The moon dipped behind a cloud and she shuddered as the darkness enveloped them, leaving her with the feeling that somewhere inside of her a similar light had been extinguished.

'I know that, in the permissive society we live in, this sort of thing is quite acceptable, but I couldn't give myself to a man unless I loved him, and knew that I was loved in return,' she said in a voice that sounded strangely flat to her ears. 'I'm sorry.'

Simon stood perfectly still, and she was thankful that he could not see the misery in her eyes.

'What game are you trying to play, Helen?' he asked finally.

'I thought you knew so much about women,' she could not help replying, biting her lip nervously as she felt, more than saw, him stiffen.

The cloud passed on, and his eyes glittered in the moonlight. 'I don't think I've ever met anyone quite like you before.'

'You told me once that I was just like all women. False and—and devious.'

'False and devious you may be,' he laughed shortly, 'but it doesn't make you less desirable.'

'Oh, please!'

She turned away from him half angrily, but stumbled over something in the darkness. His hands steadied her instantly, and then his fingers dug into her waist, drawing her closer. She raised her hands to ward him off, but, as she felt the warmth of his body through the silk of his shirt, they lingered, fascinated by the heavy beat of his heart against her palms. His mouth was in her hair, and against her throat, until he finally found her parted lips. His thighs were hard against her own, and his hands beneath her blouse brought a strange weakness to her knees, and sent an intoxicating fire racing through her bloodstream.

His kiss was a sensual exploration that awakened latent

desires, both frightening and exciting, as she floundered helplessly in her fight for sanity.

'Simon ... don't!' she pleaded against his lips as his hands slid down the length of her body, and then upwards again to the soft curve of her breasts.

'You're a witch with the brilliance of the moon in your hair, and you smell as fresh as a rose in the morning when the dew drops still clung to the petals,' he murmured, his lips warm and maddeningly persuasive against her throat.

The sound of the sea rose to a deafening roar in her ears, threatening to submerge her, and she made a final desperate effort to free herself from the spell he was casting over her.

'Please ... I must go,' she gasped, trembling as she fought against him now, and, unexpectedly, she was free, swaying slightly on her feet, and with a heart that was racing so fast it felt as though she would faint.

'Yes, go, Helen,' he said harshly, his voice lashing against tender nerves not yet recovered from his love-making. 'Go before I lose my head completely. And, next time you decide to go walking in the moonlight, let me know so that I can stay out of your way.'

Helen fled blindly across the loose sand, took the wrong path, and stumbled several times in the long grass before she reached the safety of the house. Her throat was on fire by the time she reached her room, and she fell across her bed as her limbs simply gave way beneath her, while her heart was pounding so fast that her breath came raspingly over parted lips that still tingled from the touch of that arrogant, cynical mouth.

She had so very nearly succumbed to the physical demands he had made upon her. It was a sobering thought, but if she could not possess his heart, then she wanted no part of him. She would love him always, but she would not have the memory of her love marred by indulging in a heartless affair that could last only until he tired of her, or until Rosalind had laid down her final demand.

'Oh, God,' she moaned into her pillow. 'Must I go through life knowing only the pain of loving unwisely?'

Tears brought relief, and acceptance. She had lost so much in life; her parents, Richard, and it was inevitable that there would be no place for her in Simon's life. The mere thought of him would never cease to stir the hungry yearning inside of her. The mention of his name, his photograph in the theatre column of the newspaper, or someone resembling him in appearance—all these things would keep the memory of her love alive; a love that would be of little comfort when loneliness stepped in.

'This won't do,' Helen told herself firmly as she brushed her hair out of her eyes and went through to the bathroom to run her bath water. 'To wallow in self-pity is the worst thing you could do, so snap out of it and count your blessings instead.'

Surprisingly, she went to sleep without much difficulty that night, only to awake with a start some hours later when someone shook her shoulder. She flung out an arm and switched on the bedside lamp to find Lisa standing beside her bed, the soft light falling on tousled hair, and cheeks that were damp with tears. Helen blinked at her for a moment, but the next instant she was wide awake.

'Lisa, what's the matter?' she asked anxiously, sitting up and lifting the child on to the bed. 'Have you been dreaming?'

Lisa nodded, burying her face against Helen's shoulder as the tears flowed once more. 'I'm frightened, Helen.'

'What's frightened you, my poppet?'

'I can't tell you. I promised Mummy I would never tell anyone.'

Her arms tightened involuntarily about Lisa in a protective gesture that appeared to calm the child considerably, and she held her like that for some time without speaking. Perhaps this was not the right time to probe into the past, but Helen knew, without doubt, that this poor child would have no peace until this dreadful secret was brought out into the open.

'Lisa darling,' she began gently, slipping silky strands of hair behind a small ear to expose the face that was pressed so firmly into her shoulder. 'Sometimes promises have to be broken when there's a good reason. If the promise we made is making someone very unhappy, then it's better to break that promise. You made a promise to your mummy, and that promise is making you ill and unhappy. It's also making your daddy very unhappy.' She prised the pale little face into the open, and kissed a damp cheek. 'Do you understand what I'm saying, poppet?'

'But Mummy said she would beat me,' she protested hesitantly.

Helen's throat tightened. 'Your mummy can't beat you now, darling, and if she knew how unhappy you were she wouldn't be angry with you for breaking that promise.'

Lisa's fears and doubts appeared to disintegrate slowly beneath Helen's steady gaze, but, after the months of silence, it took a considerable effort to speak of the things which had haunted her dreams to the point of hysteria. The story began haltingly, at first, then it tumbled out, and Helen listened with mounting horror until Lisa lay spent and silent in her arms.

Brenda had persuaded Simon to take the children and herself to the home of friends in the country the evening the accident had occurred. There were several guests at the wild party, and the children were eventually put to bed in one of the guest rooms. Peter, Lisa's brother, had slept soundly, but Lisa awoke with the sound of voices in the adjoining room. Presuming it to be her parents, and that it was time to return to the city, she entered the room and found her mother in the arms of a strange man. The fact that Brenda was in a partially undressed state came out quite naturally, and was fortunately of little significance to a child like Lisa, who found it far more disturbing and horrifying that her mother had been kissing a man other than her father.

Brenda was in a fury at the sight of Lisa, and thrashed her unmercifully as she extracted a promise of silence. It was at this stage that Helen understood fully why Lisa had always cried out in her sleep, begging not to be beaten, and swearing never to say a word. It was this knowledge, too, that filled Helen with a terrible anger against the woman responsible.

While Brenda had been inflicting such severe punishment on her small daughter, her companion had left the room, and this appeared to anger her more. Simon had eventually walked in on this, and an argument had resulted between Brenda and himself, which culminated in their early departure from the party. Exhausted by the beating she had received, Lisa had slept on the back seat of the car, her head cradled on her brother's lap, while he, too, slept with his head thrown back against the seat. She could not recall what had caused the accident, Lisa had said, but she awoke to find herself on the floor of the car, with Peter sprawled on the back seat. He had been cold to her touch, and she recalled covering him with a blanket. Simon was slumped unconscious against the steering wheel, but there was no sign of her mother in the car that stood with its nose buried in the ditch. Frightened because she received no response from the only two occupants in the car, she had climbed out to sit on the side of the road, crying hysterically, until a car finally pulled up beside her. The rest was vague, Lisa had explained, and Helen could only conclude that she must have fainted.

The accident, following so closely on that terrible beating, had almost succeeded in unbalancing her, Helen realised as she glanced down at the child in her arms with a tenderness that swelled warmly within her. 'You're not frightened any more, are you, Lisa?'

'Only a little,' the child owned softly, 'but I won't be if I can stay here with you. May I, Helen?'

'Of course you may,' Helen assured her warmly, taking Lisa into bed with her and switching off the light. She gathered the small, trembling bundle close to her and kissed her gently. 'It's all over now, my poppet. You don't have to be frightened again, so go to sleep, and dream about all the nice things we could do tomorrow.'

'I love you best of all, Helen,' a sleepy little voice whispered with such sincerity that Helen felt a heady warmth flow through her; a warmth that choked her momentarily and brought unashamed tears to her eyes.

'And I love you, darling Lisa,' she murmured thickly. 'Very much.'

Her burden shared, Lisa blossomed into a reasonably contented and happy child. The long, brooding silences were something of the past, and she spoke freely to Helen of the thoughts that passed through her mind. Helen gained a tremendous insight into their lives as she listened to Lisa, who had no idea just how much she was disclosing by her innocent, childish remarks and observations.

They had seldom spent time together as a family, for Brenda had always been rehearsing for a play, or was out with friends. The children had been sent to boarding school, and Simon had buried himself in his work, although Lisa could recall occasions when he had taken her out for the day, and had given her his undivided attention. Those were the happiest days Lisa could remember.

Helen never questioned Lisa, preferring instead these reminiscences to come naturally. Freedom of speech was something new to Lisa, and it brought about a marked improvement in her school work. She was an imaginative child, and displayed a vivid interest in the records Helen played for her, listening to the music and stories, and giving her own rendition afterwards. The latter became an institution eventually, and Helen did not discourage her. Children of Lisa's age needed to express themselves in this way, and Helen was often astounded at the manner in which the child enacted a story, bringing it to life with expressive gestures that displayed remarkable talent for one so young.

Simon walked into the classroom unexpectedly one morning while Lisa was enacting The Three Bears, and Helen knew at once that something was terribly wrong. His face was white, the scar on his cheek a livid red line, and his eyes black with an anger that made Helen's blood flow like ice through her veins.

'What the devil do you think you're doing?' he stormed at Lisa, and she stopped in mid-sentence, confused and frightened by the sound of his voice.

'Simon—Mr Savage,' Helen corrected herself as she went forward swiftly. 'There's really no reason for you to——'

'Is this your idea?' he interrupted harshly, turning on Helen and raking her from head to foot with eyes that were aflame with such intense hatred that she flinched and stepped back a pace as if he had struck her physically.

Lisa was crying now as she clutched at Helen's hand, and the sound of her weeping appeared to have a sobering effect on Simon, for he drew a sharp breath, and muttered something unintelligible as he sat down on his heels and drew Lisa into his arms. 'Don't cry, baby. I didn't mean to frighten you.'

He did not proceed to explain the reason for his anger, but Lisa was instantly pacified by his action, and, burying her face against his shoulder, she slipped her arms about his neck. The eyes that met Helen's over the child's head, however, had lost none of their fiery anger, and her nerves twisted into a painful knot at the pit of her stomach.

Lisa's tears evaporated and she giggled eventually at something Simon had said, but Helen had been too nervous to pay attention. He straightened eventually and towered over her, a strained look in every line of his face.

'I want to see you in my study immediately after lunch,' he instructed in a controlled voice, and an involuntary shiver made its way up her spine as she watched him stride from the room and close the door firmly behind him.

The morning had lost its sparkle as they put away the records, and closed the record player in subdued silence. They settled down to more important work, concentrating on maths, which was not Lisa's best subject, but Helen dreaded every minute that brought her closer to that confrontation with Simon.

When Bella removed their lunch trays, Helen knew that she could no longer avoid the inevitable, and, leaving Lisa on her bed with a book, she went downstairs. Pausing outside the study door, she passed a nervous hand over her hair, and knocked.

'Come in,' Simon barked, and she entered to find him standing behind his desk. 'Sit down.'

Helen sank into the nearest chair, but Simon remained standing, his manner imperious and autocratic, while his rugged face wore a grim expression that was frightening.

'Who gave you the right to encourage Lisa in that display I witnessed this morning?' he demanded without preamble.

'No one, Mr Savage, but——'

'I never asked you to include any of the theatrical arts into her curriculum, and it must stop at once.'

'But——'

'At once, do you hear?' he insisted harshly, coming round his desk to tower over her menacingly.

The muscles in his jaw knotted savagely, but Helen refused to be intimidated. 'If you could explain why, then I might understand.'

His eyes darkened. 'I don't owe you an explanation of any kind. Just do as I say.'

'You're being unreasonable, Mr Savage,' she argued, fixing her gaze on the bronze statuette of the swooping eagle rather than have her composure shattered by raising her eyes to his. 'It's the most natural thing in the world for a child of Lisa's age to play games of pretence, and to enact certain situations.'

'Is it?' he asked with heavy sarcasm. 'There must be some other way she can express herself that does not involve acting.'

'Lisa is a very talented child, and it's not surprising that she has this ability to act. I don't see why it should be suppressed——'

Helen was unprepared for what happened next, but her wrists were grasped in hands that were far from gentle, and she was yanked to her feet unceremoniously.

'That's enough!' he said through his teeth, his dark face barely inches from hers. 'In no way is she to be encouraged in this respect. Do I make myself clear?'

'Perfectly clear, Mr Savage,' she gasped, unable to bear the pain he was inflicting upon her wrists, or his intimidating nearness, much longer.

He released her just as suddenly, and she staggered slightly, gripping the edge of the desk to steady herself as she gazed ruefully at the red marks left by his fingers. She would have bruises tomorrow to remind her of this encounter, she realised.

'You may go,' he snapped, ignoring her completely as he turned away and seated himself behind his desk.

'Before I do, there's just one thing I would like to say, Mr Savage,' she said, finding it easier to speak with some distance between them. 'Lisa is not quite eight, and in the process of growing up she may decide on various occupations before finding the right one. By voicing your objections, you might just make a stage career sound more attractive.'

'Psychology, Miss Talbot?' he mocked her ruthlessly.

'No ... common sense.'

For a moment she thought that he might relent, then his

face resumed that closed expression. 'I've said all that I have to say on the subject.'

That was that! Helen thought as she made her way up to her suite, but after dinner that evening, when she returned to her lounge after putting Lisa to bed, she found Simon seated in one of the comfortable armchairs. Her heart lurched violently as she stared at him, but she recovered herself swiftly.

'Were you wanting to see me about something?' she managed calmly despite the rapid beat of the pulse at the base of her heart.

'Is this yours?' he asked, holding the small, leather bound volume of poetry in his hands which she had been reading before dinner.

'Yes,' she nodded, swallowing nervously as he opened the book.

'I read the inscription. It says: "My love, always. Richard".' His mouth twisted slightly. 'Was he your lover?'

'No.' She lowered her glance as the colour stained her cheeks. 'Richard was my fiancé.'

'Was?'

'He was killed in a landmine explosion on the border almost two years ago.'

There was a significant pause before he said: 'Care to tell me about it?'

'There's nothing much to tell,' she laughed shakily, fighting against the dreadful sensation that she would burst into tears at any moment. 'Richard and I met at the home of a mutual friend, and we sort of drifted into a relationship that was satisfying to us both. He loved me, I know, and I imagined I was in love with him at the time. We became engaged, decided on a date for the wedding, rented a flat, and then . . .' her voice trailed off into silence.

'He was called up for duty?' Simon supplied for her.

'Yes.' She ran the tip of her tongue across her dry lips, and gripped the back of a chair. 'When he died I thought it

was the end of the world, and that's why I eventually resigned my post in Cape Town and decided to look for a job
elsewhere.'

'And now you've discovered that you didn't love him at
all.' It was a statement, not a query, and there was a quality
of harshness in his voice that did not escape her.

'I loved him, yes . . . and I think we could have been very
happy together.'

'But?' he shot at her mockingly. 'There is a "but", I
presume?'

Helen raised her glance to his, her eyes a darker shade of
blue because of the wretched turmoil her emotions were in.
'I realise now that I loved him in the way I would have
loved a brother, and *not* as a woman should love the man
she hopes to marry.'

'A man like you, Simon Savage,' she told herself silently.
'But I could never be anything to you while your heart is
filled with so much hate, and while Rosalind Allen holds
that terrible sword over your head.'

'So you've actually had a lucky escape,' he remarked with
brutal frankness, and she experiencd a sickening jolt to the
stomach.

'That's a terrible thing to say when it's at the expense of
someone's life,' she exclaimed hoarsely.

He raised a satirical eyebrow. 'You're dodging the truth
again.'

Helen pulled herself up sharply. Was she merely dodging
the truth by shrinking away from a realisation she had been
too afraid to put into words? It would have been a terrible
mistake to marry Richard—she knew that now—but thinking of his death as an escape left a nasty taste in her mouth;
the taste of truth.

'You're right, I suppose,' she sighed unhappily. 'I *was*
avoiding the truth.'

'At least we agree on one thing,' he laughed briefly, and
she registered vaguely that the laughter did not quite reach

his eyes. 'Is there someone special who's made you realise that you never loved Richard?'

Her pulse quickened. 'Does there have to be someone else?'

'There usually is,' he remarked laconically. 'Toby?'

'Oh, no!' she denied fiercely, her hair a silvery cloud about her face as she shook her head. 'I could never . . .'

Her voice died in her throat as he placed the book on the arm of his chair and rose to his feet.

'You could never . . . what?'

'Love Toby,' she whispered breathlessly.

'Are you very sure of that?'

'Yes . . . very sure.'

He held her glance for a moment before he turned away and walked across to the window. The dark blue of his shirt accentuated his tan and the muscular fitness of his body as he stood with his back towards her, staring out into the darkness. There was also an elusive quality about him which she found difficult to grasp.

'About our discussion earlier today,' he said eventually, just as the silence was beginning to lengthen uncomfortably. 'You may continue to instruct Lisa as you see fit.'

This concession was surprising to say the least, but no doubt he had spent plenty of time considering the matter, and, she guessed, he was finding it difficult to admit that he was wrong. A tender smile curved her lips as she allowed her glance the freedom to dwell on his forbidding back, lingering for a moment on his dark head where the hair grew into his neck. She had never loved him more than at this moment, and it took a considerable effort not to rush to his side.

'Well?' he demanded without turning.

'Thank you, Mr Savage,' she whispered, not quite trusting herself to say more.

He turned to face her then with a look of incredulity in his eyes. 'Is that all you have to say?'

What did he expect? she wondered swiftly, lowering her lashes to veil the emotions that lay hidden in her eyes. 'What made you change your mind?'

He smiled briefly. 'Contrary to what you may believe, I do occasionally listen to advice when it's given to me, even if it does come from a slip of a girl like yourself.'

For some reason, any indication that Lisa might take after her mother had had to be crushed instantly; this much Helen understood, but she was unable to understand what had prompted this desire.

'Will it help if I promise never to encourage her too much, and treat it quite naturally?' she offered hesitantly.

'I don't want to stint Lisa's education in any way, and my objections were based on personal reasons. I really have no right to enforce my wishes on to her in this respect.' He strode about restlessly, and Helen realised only too well how much he hated having to make this confession. 'Lisa is a person in her own right, and must one day decide for herself what she wants to be. I can, I hope, guide her into avenues away from the, sometimes hard-bitten, world of acting, but in the end the choice shall be hers.' He stopped suddenly in front of her and smiled cynically. 'Your little speech certainly gave me plenty to think about.'

Helen dismissed the statement with a nervous gesture of her hands, but he captured them in his and examined the faint bruises at her wrists.

'Did I do this?' he asked in surprise, and then, when she nodded very slightly, an apologetic smile touched his lips. 'One is inclined to forget that women bruise easily.'

Helen was not quite sure what to make of his remark, but the gentle caress of his thumbs against her tender wrists created sensations she found difficult to ignore. Surely he must be aware of the rapid beat of her pulses? she thought frantically as she stared in bemused fascination at those strong hands holding hers captive with such effortless ease. She had to get away from him, she thought, with a feeling close to panic—but how? His nearness, his touch, was far too disturbing to bear without making a fool of herself once more, and right this minute she wanted his kisses more than anything in the world.

'You're trembling,' he said, and indeed she was, she discovered to her surprise. 'Do I frighten you that much?'

She closed her eyes for a moment, shutting out his image in an effort to control herself. 'Perhaps I'm just a little tired. It's been rather a long day.'

'So it has,' he agreed, releasing her. 'Goodnight, Helen.'

His touch still lingered on her wrists, but she was alone and, suddenly, very cold. His dominating presence still hovered intangibly in the room, and she wished foolishly that she could wrap it about her like a cloak.

CHAPTER NINE

THREE very disturbing weeks passed for Helen, during which Godfrey Muller, the producer, paid a visit to Brock Castle on two occasions, and she never quite knew how it happened, but she found herself acting as hostess to Simon's guest. If Godfrey Muller thought this strange, then he tactfully refrained from mentioning it, and calmly accepted Helen's presence with an affability that instantly won her liking and respect.

He was a tall man in his forties, she guessed, rather on the lean side, and with dark hair greying swiftly at the temples. Distinguished and formidable, was Helen's snap decision until she became better acquainted with him. He was an authority on the subject of the stage, and a man who knew exactly how to get the best out of the men and women who passed through his hands, but, despite his awe-inspiring exterior, he was also a very warm and compassionate man, as she discovered on his second visit to Brock Castle.

Helen served coffee on the terrace one evening, not intending to remain long, but the lights went out suddenly, plunging them into absolute darkness. Jacob appeared with two lanterns, almost as if he had expected this crisis and, after placing one on the small table, he and Simon disappeared into the house to locate the fuse box, leaving Helen alone with Godfrey.

'You're in love with him, aren't you?' the question came without warning, and Helen's empty cup rattled dangerously in its saucer as she placed it on the tray. A denial hovered on her lips, but Godfrey forestalled her with an astonishing astuteness that sent the colour rushing painfully to her cheeks. 'It's no use denying it, my dear,' he said calmly. 'You have very expressive eyes, and they've told me far more than you might have wished.'

'Oh, dear,' Helen sighed helplessly, all desire to argue away the truth deserting her. 'Am I so terribly transparent?'

'To me, yes. It's my business to know people, but Simon is too busy with his own problems to notice anything beyond the fact that you're a beautiful woman,' Godfrey frowned, neatly clipping off the end of one of his cigars, and lighting it carefully. 'I sometimes think it will take an earthquake to shatter the wall he's built around himself. You never met Brenda, did you?'

'No, but I saw her on the stage once or twice,' Helen replied, in the grip of a frightening expectancy as she sat facing him in the lamplight with her hands clenched in her lap. 'What was she like?'

'On stage she was one of the finest actresses it was ever my good fortune to meet,' he smiled reminiscently, then his face hardened. 'Offstage she was as destructive as the asp that supposedly killed Cleopatra. No man, whether he was married or not, could apparently resist her, and during the last three years of her life she often used alcohol and drugs abusively.'

A shiver of shock went through her. 'Was Simon aware of this?'

'I'm almost positive that he was, but it made no difference. Neither he nor Brenda hid the fact that their marriage was no longer a real one, and had not been so since Brenda knew that she was expecting Lisa.'

'But why?'

'That's the burning question, as they say,' he laughed slightly, embarrassed by his own turn of phrase. 'They appeared to be reasonably happy during those first years, then, suddenly, they were hardly ever seen together. Brenda no longer camouflaged the fact that she enjoyed the company of other men, and Simon worked harder, burning himself out and, in the process, becoming the hard and embittered man he is today.'

The pleasant aroma of his Havana cigar lingered in the air as she asked tentatively, 'Were there ever any other women in his life?'

'Several before his marriage, but afterwards? ... no.' His formidable features creased into a smile that made her realise the pitiful transparency of her question. 'I've come to the conclusion that he's lost his appetite for women completely, or perhaps ... not quite.'

His slight hesitation brought another, more urgent, thought to mind. 'How does Rosalind Allen fit into the picture?'

'Oh, Rosalind...' He gestured expressively with his hands as if he found the mention of her name distasteful. 'For years she lived in her sister's shadow, hoping to match Brenda's capabilities on the stage, but with not enough talent to gain more than a minor role. She clung to Brenda like a veritable leech, and now that Brenda is no longer there, she has attached herself to Simon in the same way, hoping, I suppose, that she might at least have some success in becoming the next Mrs Simon Savage.'

His dismissal of Rosalind's talents was almost brutal, but then, she supposed, someone in his position had to be brutal at times. 'You make it sound dreadfully cold-blooded, and somehow pathetic.'

'Life *is* like that occasionally,' he reminded her gently.

'Yes, I suppose so.' The thought of Rosalind stepping into Brenda's shoes as Simon's wife was painfully alarming, but the possibility was not so remote considering the hold Rosalind had over him. Helen groaned inwardly, voicing her fears. 'Do you think she might succeed in becoming his wife?'

'I hope not!' Godfrey exploded just as the lights came on again, and he stared at his cigar as if he wondered how it had got there between his fingers. 'It would be like piling one disaster upon another.'

'What would be like piling one disaster upon another?' a deep voice asked suddenly from the doorway, and Helen's nerve ends tightened as she wondered frantically how much Simon had heard of their conversation.

She stared at Godfrey, but he appeared quite unperturbed as he replied, 'If the leading lady in your play took ill on the opening night, and the understudy collapsed with an attack of nerves.'

Helen applauded him silently, and almost burst out laughing as she caught the wicked gleam in his eyes.

'In that case you should perhaps put Helen in the role of the understudy's understudy, if you'll pardon the expression,' Simon announced dryly, his dark eyes taking in Helen's flushed cheeks. 'She would be perfect as Marilyn in many ways.'

The silence was all at once electrifying. What exactly had he meant by that? she wondered confusedly, groping for an explanation as she glanced at Godfrey's strangely still form in the chair opposite.

'I think not, Simon,' the producer said at last, and there was silent disapproval in his grey eyes.

Unable to find an answer for that tense moment on the terrace, Helen dismissed the incident from her mind with the explanation that she was over-imaginative.

Rosalind arrived on one of her flying visits to Brock Castle the following weekend, and the two days passed swiftly and pleasantly enough, except for one unfortunate incident shortly after her arrival.

Lisa and Helen had arrived back from the village to find Rosalind sunbathing on the terrace. In her strapless lemon creation her perfectly moulded shoulders glistened in the sun, while the hem of her dress had been raised to well above her knees to expose long, shapely, and equally tanned legs. She rose instantly the moment they stepped on to the terrace and greeted Lisa effusively, but Lisa was not fooled —children seldom are—and she remained stiffly and silently in her aunt's embrace.

'What's the matter? Aren't you glad to see me?' Rosalind demanded sharply, holding Lisa a little way from her.

'No,' Lisa replied without hesitation.

She had been candid to the point of rudeness, but before Helen could reprimand her, Rosalind had pushed her away, her eyes green flames of anger. 'You're a very naughty and rude little girl, and I have a good mind to see to it that your daddy gives you the beating you deserve.'

Lisa's bottom lip quivered slightly as she glanced up at Helen. 'I'm going up to my room.'

'Yes, go up to your room,' Rosalind agreed coldly, 'and stay there until you're ready to apologise. Not you!' she added, her nails digging into Helen's arm as she was about to follow Lisa. 'I want a word with you.'

Helen glanced down at the long-fingered hand with the carefully tinted nails, and said coldly, 'Take your hand off my arm.'

The hand was removed instantly, but four dents remained as a reminder. 'You are to blame for the child's behaviour.'

'I beg your pardon?'

'Don't look so innocent with me, Miss Talbot. You know what I'm talking about.'

'I assure you I've never encouraged Lisa to behave in this manner towards you.'

That beautifully shaped mouth curved sardonically. 'You would be well advised not to, for I shall have no hesitation in slapping her into boarding school the moment Simon and I are married.'

Recalling Godfrey's statement, Helen hovered between pity and fear, and a large amount of anger. 'That wouldn't solve the problem, Miss Allen.'

'Perhaps not,' Rosalind agreed, inspecting her nails with a careless expression on her usually hard face, 'but it will keep her out of my way most of the time. Simon's flat isn't big enough for the three of us, and that dreadful dog of Lisa's will have to go as well.'

She made their marriage sound so definite that Helen felt a chill about her heart which she was certain would never disperse. 'Have you discussed this with Simon?'

Those beautifully arched eyebrows were raised a fraction. 'Naturally.'

'I see.'

The day lost its warmth and Helen suppressed a shiver. So Simon had allowed himself to be blackmailed into this marriage after all. Or had he perhaps suggested it willingly? Helen rejected the latter swiftly. Simon would never allow himself to be fooled twice, so it could only mean that he had finally agreed to pay the price.

'I did warn you that our marriage was inevitable,' Rosalind's voice cut through her thoughts.

'So you did,' Helen murmured, and, with a muttered excuse she entered the house, relying on the remnants of her composure to carry her up the stairs to her suite.

'I hate her!' Lisa exclaimed, emerging from the depths of a chair as Helen entered.

'You shouldn't say that,' Helen reprimanded, her voice sounding strained.

'I can't help it, it's true.'

Helen drew her towards the small sofa and they sat down facing each other. 'You *were* very rude, Lisa.'

The dark head drooped slightly. 'I know, and I'm sorry ... but I know she doesn't really like me either.'

'How can you be so sure of that?' Helen sighed, crossing her fingers unobtrusively. 'If you would only give her the opportunity you may discover that she is very fond of you.'

'She isn't fond of me. I know she isn't,' Lisa cried agitatedly. 'But I know what she wants. She wants to marry

Daddy, and then I'll have to be nice to her because she'll be my new mommy.'

Helen felt as though every ounce of breath had been squeezed from her lungs. There was very little that escaped Lisa, and she was far more perceptive than anyone guessed.

'Would that be so terrible?' she asked finally.

'Yes, yes, it would,' Lisa nodded emphatically, flinging herself unexpectedly into Helen's arms. 'Oh, Helen! Why don't you marry Daddy, then you could be my mommy. I would rather have *you* for a mommy than anyone else in the world.'

It was the highest compliment Lisa could ever have paid her, but to Helen it was like a blow to the heart. 'Thank you for saying that, my poppet, but I couldn't marry your daddy.'

Lisa's eyes widened in dismay. 'Why not?'

'Well, people don't just get married, Lisa. They have to love each other,' Helen explained, priding herself on the fact that her voice sounded perfectly steady.

'Don't you love Daddy, then?'

'Oh, yes, yes, I *do* love him,' her heart cried wildly, but aloud she said: 'I ... like and respect your daddy very much.'

'But, if you tried hard enough, you could love him, couldn't you?' Lisa persisted, unaware of the strain she was placing on Helen at that moment with her innocent queries.

'Oh, Lisa,' Helen laughed shakily, and very close to tears, 'if only it were all as simple as that!'

Lisa buried her head against Helen's shoulder, and, fortunately, Helen's tearful state went unnoticed as she laid her cheek against the dark head pressed so tightly against her.

'Don't you want to be my mommy?'

Lisa's muffled query hurt deeply, and Helen's arms tightened involuntarily about the slight little figure in an unconscious effort to mitigate the pain that was searing through her soul.

'I would give anything in the world to be your mummy, but——'

Lisa wriggled herself out of Helen's arms. 'Then why don't you tell Daddy?'

'No!'

Lisa's uncomprehending frown deepened. 'But, Helen——'

'Lisa, darling ... please,' she begged as a wave of helpless longing threatened to dislodge the tears she was struggling so valiantly to restrain.

'Oh, all right,' Lisa agreed unhappily, disengaging herself and walking towards her room with a wounded expression in her eyes as she added in a mumbling tone, 'Why must grown-ups always be so difficult?'

Helen sagged against the sofa and closed her eyes against the flow of tears. 'Oh, Simon, Simon,' she moaned softly. 'Why did I have to come here, of all places, to look for a job? Why couldn't I have gone to some nice obscure little place where there would have been no danger of ever knowing you?'

The opening night of Simon's play *Chains of Freedom* was scheduled for the first week in December, and a few days before the time they travelled in Simon's Bentley to the home of Godfrey Muller.

'I've arranged for you and Lisa to stay here with Godfrey and Corinne,' Simon explained as he drove through the pillared gates, and up the long drive to the gabled house she glimpsed through the trees. 'I shall be staying at my flat in town.'

Helen did not question this, for the Dutch-styled house, with its sloping white gables and thatched roof, drew her attention, and she knew that one day, if the opportunity ever presented itself, she would want to live in a house similar to this, amid lawns and trees, and nestled against the rising slopes of Table Mountain.

'It's beautiful,' Simon agreed in a strangely relaxed voice. 'Every time I come here I'm aware of the beauty and tranquillity of the place. Corinne is one of the most remarkable women I've ever known, for she's managed to capture some of that tranquillity in her home as well.'

This sounded odd, coming from Simon, but the moment she saw Corinne Muller coming down the slatted steps to welcome them, she knew what Simon had meant.

There was an air of peace and serenity about Corinne that was almost tangible. She was small and slender for her forty years, with titian hair that showed almost no sign of greying, and blue eyes that mirrored a radiance that came from deep within. She was a mixture of sophistication and simplicity, with a charm that would set the most nervous guest at ease.

She welcomed Helen as if she were part of the family, and they were swept into the cool interior of the house with its spacious rooms, and carefully selected antiques which blended in perfectly with the more modern furnishings. Nothing jarred in this house, was Helen's first impression, for Corinne had chosen restful shades of autumn for the living-room, and the palest lemon for the rooms Helen and Lisa were to occupy.

A tray of tea awaited their return to the living-room, and Lisa, a little lost without Scampy, made her way into the garden eventually.

'Godfrey is waiting for you at the theatre,' Corinne told Simon in her lilting voice as he placed his cup in the tray and prepared to leave. 'And, Simon, be sure to have him home before seven this evening. You know how he gets carried away when the opening night is close at hand.'

Simon smiled briefly. 'I'll do my best, but don't we all get a little carried away at a time like this?'

'Oh, dear,' Corinne murmured without rancour. 'I can see another splendid dinner being ruined.'

'I shan't willingly miss one of your dinners, Corinne,' he remarked, nodding coolly in Helen's direction. 'See you later.'

'Not later than seven,' Corinne laughed, turning to Helen the moment they were alone. 'Relax, my dear. Lisa can come to no harm in the garden, and I'm hoping you'll join me in a second cup of tea.'

That first afternoon spent with Corinne was the only truly peaceful time for Helen during their stay in Cape Town. One way or another they were all swept up in the preparations and mounting tension of the opening night. The most embarrassing moment for Helen was when they retired to the living-room after dinner on the last evening before the play was to open.

The discussion, naturally, revolved around *Chains of Freedom*, and after living with it for so long, it was not unusual that a certain element of doubt should prevail.

'Don't get the last-minute jitters,' Corinne warned the two men. 'It will be a wonderful success, and after tomorrow night, Helen and I will give you our valued opinion, won't we, Helen?'

'I think they'll have to rely on your opinion alone, Corinne,' Helen replied calmly. 'I shall be staying with Lisa.'

'Nonsense!' Corinne exploded after a tense little silence. 'One of the servants can stay in and keep an eye on her, so there's no reason for you to miss this occasion.'

'Helen hasn't a very high opinion of my work, Corinne,' Simon remarked lazily. 'Perhaps she doesn't want to go.'

Helen's glance was unwavering as it met Simon's. 'I would like to go very much, but I didn't think you would want me to leave Lisa.'

'Lisa will be quite safe here with Corinne's servants.'

'That's settled, then,' Corinne remarked happily.

'Not quite,' Helen replied, her cheeks suffused with

colour as she wrenched her glance from Simon's. 'I haven't anything appropriate to wear, I'm afraid.'

Corinne was not baulked by this statement at all. 'But then you and I must go shopping tomorrow, and I think I know just the place where you'll find something to suit your taste.'

'I'm in a generous mood tonight, so buy whatever you want, Helen, and have the account sent to me,' Simon said, extracting a cigarette from the slim gold case he always carried with him, and lighting it.

'There now,' Corinne remarked excitedly. 'It isn't often that a woman receives an offer like that, so say "yes" quickly, Helen, before he changes his mind.'

Embarrassment quickened her pulse as she met the undisguised mockery in those dark eyes. 'Thank you, Simon.'

Godfrey, who had been following the conversation with silent reserve, rose from his chair. 'Now that Corinne and Simon have organised your immediate future to the last detail, may I offer you a sherry?'

'Thank you,' Helen murmured with a smile as she glanced up into clear eyes that held a hint of mischief and understanding.

'And you, my dear, a dry sherry?' he asked, placing a hand on his wife's shoulder.

Corinne raised her hand to his briefly and nodded.

'Come and help yourself, Simon,' Godfrey suggested, strolling across to the teak cabinet at the other end of the room.

Helen did not dare look up as Simon passed her chair, but her heart almost stopped as his hand tugged at her hair and forced her to raise her face to his. There was a very subtle softening in the harsh lines of his face, but the expression in his eyes remained unfathomable.

'I shall expect an honest and unbiased opinion tomorrow night,' he told her abruptly. 'Don't forget.'

*

Dressed in the flowing silk gown with its various shades of blue which she had bought at Corinne's insistence despite the price, Helen inspected herself in the full-length mirror and had to admit that she had made the right choice. The gown exposed shoulders which had acquired a golden tan during the hours spent on the beach with Lisa, and the soft material clung gently to the curve of her breasts, and her slender, supple waist. She had left her hair loose to fall in a soft cloud on to her shoulders, and had taken a little extra care with her make-up.

She wanted to look her best for Simon, but she somehow doubted whether her appearance would impress him in any way. His heart was hardened against women, and besides ... there was Rosalind.

'Are you ready?' Corinne asked, entering the room in a flowing cream-coloured creation that gave her an almost regal quality, then she stopped and brought her hands together in a slightly theatrical gesture. 'Helen, you look beautiful! I just knew that the colour would bring out the extraordinary shade of your hair to perfection.'

Helen coloured slightly. 'Would you believe me if I told you I'm nervous?'

Corinne's blue glance softened perceptibly. 'When someone you love is involved in something important to his career, then it's quite natural to be nervous. I'm just as nervous for Godfrey's sake.'

Before Helen could reply to this surprising statement, there was a knock at the door and Simon entered.

'Godfrey and I are on our way,' he informed them, his eyes glittering strangely as they briefly took in Helen's appearance. 'Will the two of you manage on your own?'

'Of course, Simon,' Corinne said reassuringly. 'We'll be there long before the curtain rises.'

After another brief glance in Helen's direction, he nodded, and they were once more alone.

'There goes another impossible man who needs the gentle

touch of a woman's hand to temper the angry fire within him.'

'Another impossible man?' Helen asked nervously.

'Yes, my dear,' Corinne smiled with a reminiscent look in her blue eyes. 'In some ways Simon and Godfrey are very much alike. I met Godfrey when he produced a play in which I played the leading role. We clashed from the moment we set eyes on each other, and I remember thinking him the most impossible and heartless man I'd ever met. But the heart has a mind of its own, and I ended up by falling so desperately in love with him that I was absolutely miserable until I discovered that, by some miracle, he loved me too.' She laughed with a hint of embarrassment at disclosing so much. 'It was only after he opened his arms and his heart to me that I became acquainted with the real Godfrey Muller, and discovered that he was really a very sensitive and wonderful man.'

Helen fingered her silver evening bag with an ache in her heart. 'Do you think Simon would ever allow any woman close enough to accomplish such a miracle?'

'If she was the right woman, yes,' Corinne nodded emphatically. 'Godfrey told me quite a lot about you. He's a very good judge of character, but now that I've met you personally, I know he was right.' She touched Helen's arm to stress her statement. 'You've done wonders with Lisa, Helen, and I just know you could do the same for Simon.'

'If only he would let me,' Helen thought miserably. 'If only ...' She pulled herself together sharply. 'It's wonderful of you to say so, but I think Simon has made up his mind to marry Rosalind.'

Corinne paled slightly. 'If he did *that*, then he would go down drastically in my estimation. He's not a fool, Helen.'

'No, but he may have no choice.'

There was a significant silence before Corinne said calmly, 'Well, I'm not sure I know what you mean by that, but personally I don't think Rosalind stands a chance.'

There was no time to continue the discussion, and after a last look at Lisa to make sure that she was asleep, they drove to the theatre.

Helen had known that Godfrey had acquired the use of Cape Town's newest theatre for Simon's play, but she was still dazzled by the lights and the splendour of her surroundings as she walked with Corinne through the crowd of expensively dressed patrons in the large, plushly furnished foyer. Corinne stopped occasionally to speak to some of the imposing personalities in the theatre world, introducing Helen as a close friend of Simon's, and ignoring the growing dismay in Helen's glances. There was no sign of Simon or Godfrey, but this did not appear to trouble Corinne when they finally entered the auditorium and were shown to their places in the front row of the circle with a clear view of the stage.

Helen felt rather out of place in the most expensive seats instead of further towards the back where ordinary mortals, like herself, could afford the price on opening nights.

'Will Simon and Godfrey be joining us?' she whispered to Corinne.

'Not if I know those two,' Corinne replied with a soft laugh. 'They'll most probably hide themselves backstage somewhere to pamper their anxieties while they watch the play, and note every reaction in the audience.'

When the lights were finally dimmed to signify that the play was about to begin, Helen's nerves were so tightly coiled that the programme shook in her hands. Corinne smiled encouragingly, but Helen noticed that she, too, had an unusually tense expression on her soft features. There was a hush in the auditorium as the curtain rose, and from that moment onwards, Helen was aware only of the dramatic events taking place on the stage.

As the plot unveiled itself through the characters, she realised that it could in many ways be Simon's own story. The love, hate, and final disillusionment moved Helen from a state of shocked awareness to unashamed tears, and when the ruthless Marilyn finally died at the hands of an irate lover, the entire audience appeared to collapse with a sigh of relief—but this was not the end. Marilyn's husband had gained the freedom he so desperately desired, only to discover that he was imprisoned by the chains of bitterness which surrounded him, and from this there was no escape, except in the arms of the shadowy woman who dominated the final scene by representing a capacity for the love and warmth which had, till that moment, seemed like an impossible dream.

As the final curtain came down Helen felt drained of all emotion. She had risen to her feet with everyone else when Simon had appeared on the stage with the cast to acknowledge the thunderous applause, but there was a dreadful sensation at the pit of her stomach that made her wish she could escape unnoticed to a place where she could hide for ever.

The only clear thought in her mind at that moment was Simon's remark to Godfrey Muller on the night the lights had failed at Brock Castle. 'She would be perfect as Marilyn in many ways.'

Was that how he saw her? A ruthless, calculating woman who would stop at nothing to gain from life what she desired, regardless of the unhappiness she caused those closest to her?

No, no! It was impossible! He could not think of her like that after all these months she had lived under the same roof with him? They had argued about certain things, yes, and he had made love to her a little on two occasions. Surely he was not filled with such hatred and bitterness that he could still think of her in such a way?

'Helen...' Corinne's hand was on her arm. 'The men will be expecting us to go backstage, and——' She stopped suddenly when she noticed Helen's deathly pallor. 'Are you feeling ill, my dear?'

'No ... no, I'm all right.'

'Simon's play was very moving, I admit.'

'Yes ... very,' Helen agreed as they made their way through a side door into the foyer.

Godfrey's lean figure emerged from the throng of people wishing to congratulate the cast, and one look at his usually formidable features told them that he was more than satisfied with that evening's performance, and the ovation they had received.

With his arm about Corinne's shoulders, he said: 'I wouldn't go backstage, if I were you. Simon and I are a bit tied up with the press at the moment, so I think the two of you should go home and await our guests. We'll follow you as soon as we can.'

Helen's relief at not coming face to face with Simon at that moment was indescribable. She would have time to compose herself, and to decide on what she would say when he eventually demanded her opinion, as he undoubtedly would. Corinne was equally silent during the trip back to the house, and Helen could only imagine that her thoughts still dwelled on the play, as would be the case with everyone else who had sat through the dramatic events of the past three hours. There was no doubt about it that Simon's play, *Chains of Freedom*, had been a resounding success, and would continue to be so for as long as the public demanded its showing, but to Helen the masterpiece Simon had created was spoiled by the echo of his accusation; for an accusation it had undoubtedly been, Helen acknowledged to herself.

Lisa was still sleeping peacefully when they arrived at Corinne's lovely home, and, while the stream of guests arrived, Helen escaped to her bedroom for a few moments of solitude, but from the window of her darkened room she saw Simon's silver Bentley come up the drive, and from that moment her heart beat out an irregular tattoo that refused to be stilled. She did not want to have to face

Simon. How could she, when every part of her felt bruised by the painful knowledge she had acquired?

There was a light tap at her door some minutes later, and she called, 'Come in, Corinne.'

But it was not Corinne who entered and snapped on the light. It was Simon; tall and lean, and with that aura of masculinity about him that never failed to stir her senses. His white shirt contrasted vividly with the darkness of his evening suit, and his tanned complexion, while his tight-lipped expression awakened a frightened pulse at the base of her throat as he came towards her. She tried to escape the silent fury in his eyes, but they held her own captive for breathless seconds while she struggled to understand the reason for his threatening attitude.

'Well?' he demanded harshly with that savage twist to his lips. 'Was there absolutely nothing in that play that made any sense to you? Is that why you're hiding up here in your room, because you can't face me with the truth?'

Helen drew a halting breath. 'I wasn't hiding from you, Simon.'

'Really?' his eyebrows rose a fraction. 'Then why weren't you downstairs when I arrived?'

'I came up to check on Lisa, and then I—I wanted to be alone for a moment.'

'Why?'

'To think about your play, mainly.'

'And?'

'It was outstanding,' she managed eventually, fascinated by the nerve jumping beneath the scarred tissue on his cheek.

'Is that all?'

'Was there supposed to be something else?' she asked, her temples throbbing painfully.

'No,' he snapped coldly. 'If there was nothing in the play that was of any significance to you, then I underestimated you completely.'

'I don't think I understand,' she whispered confusedly, pressing her fingers against her aching temples.

'No, you don't,' he agreed harshly, 'but perhaps you'll understand *this*.'

He caught her roughly against him, pinning her arms at her sides with his own before his mouth bruised hers until the tears finally forced their way between her lashes and slid down her cheeks. His lips and his arms were a punishment, and she was close to fainting when he finally released her, but it was only when he closed the door firmly behind him that she opened her eyes, and took the weight off her trembling legs by sinking into the chair behind her.

peared behind the trees, leaving her with the despairing realisation that the barrier between them had been strengthened severely.

Nothing seemed the same after that. They drove back to Strafford on the Sunday morning with an absolute silence between them and, had it not been for Lisa's occasional chatter, Helen would have burst into tears. She had become accustomed to Simon's mockery and cynicism in the past, but his cold indifference was more painful than anything she had experienced before.

If she could only have explained the reason for her behaviour, she thought frantically, but why would he believe her when he had such a cast-iron opinion of her character?

The atmosphere at Brock Castle, just before Christmas, could be explained only as intolerable, and Helen often escaped to the beach with Lisa where they could spend a few carefree hours with Scampy in the surf. Aunt Ada, too, was thrilled by the many visits they paid her during this time, and although she remarked on the faint shadows gathering beneath Helen's eyes, they were never explained, for Helen stoically avoided discussing her problems.

She saw Toby often during those two weeks, but she hated herself for making use of his friendship as a method of escape from her own unhappiness. He made no secret of the way he felt about her; it was there in every glance, and every touch, but somehow she did not have the heart, nor the will, to refuse his invitations. His attentiveness was balm to her bruised heart at that time, but soon she would have to break off their relationship—for *his* sake more than anything else.

Toby invited her to have dinner with him again one evening, and she had made up her mind before the time that this would be her opportunity to speak to him, but facing him across the dinner table, the words locked in her throat, and she was forced to remain silent. The opportunity presented itself, finally, when they drove home that night. Toby had parked his car on a rise just above Strafford, and they sat for a time watching the sea shimmering in the moonlight.

'I presume Lisa will be going to boarding school next year?' Toby remarked while Helen was still struggling to find the right words with which to begin.

'I suppose so, yes.'

'How long do you still have to remain at Brock Castle?'

'Just until after New Year. Why?'

Foolish question, she chided herself, when she had a very shrewd idea where the conversation was heading.

'Have you made any plans for the future?'

'No.' She could delay it no longer, she decided as she turned to face him, but Toby was determined to have his say.

'Helen, we've known each other some months now, and——'

'You're a very dear friend, Toby, and I shall miss you when I leave Strafford,' she interrupted swiftly, hoping desperately that he would take the hint, but he remained unusually dense.

'You don't have to leave. You could marry me.'

'I—I don't think——'

'You must have guessed that I love you, Helen,' he said urgently, his hand touching her shoulder as he leaned towards her to search her face in the darkness.

Helen felt like a criminal as she moved slightly beyond his reach, but it had to be said. 'Yes, I know, and I'm sorry.'

'Does that mean——?'

'It means that I'm terribly honoured that you should feel this way about me, but I couldn't marry you without loving you, Toby,' she told him gently, hating the glimmer of pain on his dear face. 'I'm very fond of you, but...' her voice trailed off into silence, and she swallowed with difficulty.

Toby moved away from her then and lit a cigarette, something he seldom did. 'Is there someone else?' he asked after a long silence.

'Yes ... but nothing will ever come of it,' she explained, realising that, after refusing his offer of marriage, she at least owed him the truth.

'Simon Savage?' he asked then, and, as she nodded, he sighed heavily. 'I thought so.' Again there was that long silence before he asked, 'Does he know how you feel about him?'

'No,' she admitted with a little laugh that became strangled in her throat. 'I'm afraid it's a completely one-sided affair.'

Toby crushed his cigarette into the ashtray, and turned to face her once more with that same urgency he had displayed some minutes ago. 'Helen, my dear, why waste your time with a man like that who couldn't appreciate you if he tried? We *could* be happy together if we tried.'

He was kissing her then, but she knew, just as he did, that it was hopeless, and if nothing else would have convinced him, then her unresponsive lips finally did.

'Toby, you will always be a very dear friend to me,' she whispered when he released her, 'but I couldn't marry you feeling the way I do about—about someone else. It wouldn't be fair to you because you deserve to be happy.'

'Very well, Helen,' he said at length, striving at a smile, and not quite succeeding. 'But remember ... I'll always be there if you should need me.'

She leaned forward impulsively then, and kissed him lightly on the cheek. 'I shall remember that, Toby, and ... thank you.'

They were driving through the village some minutes later when Helen caught a brief glimpse of a car parked at Aunt Ada's gate. Her heart somersaulted violently, for the car had been, unmistakably, Simon's! No one in the district owned anything as spectacular as a Bentley, and certainly none of her aunt's friends in the city possessed one. But what could he possibly want with Aunt Ada, and why this sudden desire to become acquainted?

The gates of Brock Castle swung open and Toby drove through, but, as Helen said goodnight moments later, she had already made up her mind to pay a visit to her aunt to discover the reason behind Simon's presence there that night.

The moment she was free the following evening, Helen drove to Aunt Ada's cottage, and there, in the homely atmosphere of the kitchen, she decided to confront her aunt.

'I had dinner last night with Toby in the restaurant of the new motel they've opened just out of town,' she began, placing her elbows on the scrubbed table, and resting her chin in her hands as she watched her aunt pouring the tea. 'On our way back I noticed you had a visitor.'

Solid, dependable Aunt Ada, who was seldom flustered by anything, all at once appeared to have some difficulty with the tea strainer. 'Yes ... Mr Savage's visit was most unexpected.'

'What did he want?'

'Oh, he talked about Lisa mostly,' her aunt said casually; almost too casually as she fussed with the milk and the sugar bowl. 'He said he was pleased with the way her health had improved, and asked about the local school as there was a slight possibility that he might make Brock Castle his permanent home.'

This contradicted Rosalind's statement that he would soon return to the city, Helen thought, her spirits down to zero as she somehow summoned a smile. 'I can't see Rosalind giving up her life in the city to settle here in Strafford.'

'Rosalind?'

'Rosalind Allen,' Helen explained, helping herself to milk and sugar, and stirring her tea thoughtfully. 'She's Lisa's aunt, and the woman he's going to marry. Didn't he tell you that?'

Aunt Ada's grey eyes registered surprise and something else which was indefinable. 'Well ... yes, he did mention something about getting married.'

So, Helen thought dismally, it was decided. Rosalind had finally persuaded him into a marriage that could only be as disastrous as his first. Simon was a fool! she thought, wincing inwardly at the pain searing through her. And *she* was an even bigger fool for loving him!

'Poor Simon...' her thoughts continued, '... and poor Lisa.'

'Why do you say that?' Her aunt's startled voice made her realise that she had spoken out aloud.

'Oh, it's nothing,' she shrugged, loath to explain just how deeply she was affected by the knowledge her aunt had imparted. 'What do you think of him now that you've met him?'

'He's a very pleasant man to talk to, and not at all the pompous character I thought him,' her aunt said enthusiastically. 'It's a pity about that scar on his face, though.'

'Yes.'

'But it doesn't exactly mar his good looks.'

'No.'

'Oh, Simon, Simon, why did I have to love you like this?' she thought as she fought desperately against the desire to weep on the comforting shoulder of the woman seated opposite her.

'Have you decided yet what you're going to do when you leave Brock Castle?' Aunt Ada's voice interrupted her thoughts.

Helen bit her lip agitatedly. 'No, I haven't.'

Aunt Ada's hand on her arm was comforting, but there was a certain urgency in the firmness of her grip. 'Don't be too hasty, my dear. There's plenty of time to decide on your future.'

It was a strange remark coming from her aunt, who had always insisted, in the past, that decisions had to be made at once, and not shelved indefinitely, but Helen was too distraught to notice the significance at that moment.

Rosalind arrived at Brock Castle the day before Christmas, announcing that she intended to stay until after New Year, and, observing Simon's expression on her arrival, Helen noticed that he gave no indication whether this pleased him or not. Determined to avoid them as much as possible, Helen went down to join Lisa and Scampy in the garden. The intention was to keep Lisa out of her aunt's way, but, as Helen stepped into the hall, Lisa came dashing past her in a near hysterical state.

'Lisa!' she called after the child, and then, when she was about to follow her, Rosalind stepped inside through the front entrance. Helen turned to her instantly and demanded anxiously, 'What happened?'

Rosalind surveyed her with a certain insolence. 'I don't know that it has anything to do with you, but I told her you would soon be leaving, and that it was arranged for her to go to boarding school next year.'

'You did what?' Helen asked incredulously.

'Well, she had to be told some time, you know, and the sooner the better, I say,' Rosalind remarked casually, but there was no mistaking the look of self-satisfaction in her glittering green eyes.

A wave of anger swept over Helen which she found almost impossible to control. Never in her life had she felt so much like doing someone a physical injury. 'Rosalind Allen,' she said with a deadly calm, 'if you have destroyed all my hard work during the past months by upsetting that child, I swear I'll make you regret it for the rest of your life!'

'May I know what's going on?' Simon's deep voice demanded behind her, and she swung round to face him, her blue eyes dark with unaccustomed rage.

'Ask *her*!' she almost shouted, pointing at Rosalind, who

seemed quite unperturbed by the damage she had done, and then, unable to bear the sight of either of them a moment longer, she brushed past Simon and went up the stairs two at a time in her urgency to find Lisa.

She found her lying in a crumpled heap on the sofa in her lounge, her slight body shaking with uncontrollable sobs.

'Lisa darling, don't cry,' she exclaimed, gathering the child into her arms and comforting her. 'It breaks my heart to see you cry like this.'

'She—she said you were g-going away, and that I was going to b-boarding school,' Lisa sobbed into her shoulder, her one hand clutching desperately at the front of Helen's silk blouse. 'Say it isn't so, Helen. Say it isn't so!'

Helen's arms tightened about her as she swallowed convulsively. 'Lisa, calm yourself. You'll only make yourself ill if you carry on in this way.'

'Helen, I don't mind so much about going to boarding school, but promise me you won't go away. Promise me you'll stay?'

Helen brushed the dark strands of hair from the child's tear-wet face, as she had done so often in the past, and wished with every part of her being that she could have given Lisa the assurance she desired.

'Darling, you're well again, and I shall have to look for a job elsewhere,' she told her gently.

'You could still stay here,' Lisa cried, raising her flushed little face to Helen's. 'If I really have to go to boarding school, then I will, but you must be here when I come home for the holidays, so please don't go away, Helen. Please!'

'You're not going to boarding school, and Helen's not going anywhere, Lisa baby. She's staying right here where she belongs.'

Neither of them had heard Simon enter, but Helen's nerve ends tightened as she looked up into those dark, unfathomable eyes. What was he trying to do? Prolong the inevitable? Then an alarming thought took shape in her mind. If Simon was expecting her to remain and witness his marriage to Rosalind, then he could think again. No! Never would she remain here to see *that* happening. Not even for Lisa's sake would she consider it.

'Do you mean that, Daddy?' she heard Lisa asking hesitantly.

'Every word.'

'Yippee!' Lisa shouted, her tears drying miraculously as she jumped to her feet and bounced up and down.

Helen's heart felt like a piece of lead inside her as she watched this display of exuberance. How could he be so cruel? she wondered distractedly, for there was no sign of remorse in his glance as it met hers briefly.

'Now, get yourself down to the kitchen,' he told Lisa calmly. 'Rosie is baking your favourite biscuits, and I'm sure she won't mind if you sample a few.'

Lisa bounced across to Helen, hugged her profusely, and then hurried quite contentedly from the room.

Helen was only vaguely aware of a car crunching on the gravel beneath her window during the uneasy silence which followed Lisa's departure. Then she rose to her feet and straightened her skirt with unsteady hands. 'How could you tell her I would be staying, when you know that it isn't true?'

'I *want* you to stay, Helen,' he said. 'Permanently.'

She stared at him for a moment, her harsh reply dying on her lips as she felt the familiar quickening of her pulse at the sight of him. Would she ever be able to divest her mind and heart of this love she had for him? she wondered frantically. She would have done anything for him, but to expect her to remain in this house with Rosalind and himself would be more than any human could bear.

'I *can't* stay here!' she heard herself say on a note of desperation. 'It's out of the question!'

'I know you're very fond of Lisa,' he remarked, his

shoulders moving slightly beneath the expensive cotton of his white shirt. 'Am *I* the one you find so repulsive?'

'No! I don't find you repulsive, I...'

There was an unbearable tension between them, and something else that made Helen feel as though she were about to be hurled over the edge of a cliff. She held her breath, not daring to raise her glance higher than the top button of his shirt where the dark hair on his chest was only just visible.

'I want you, Helen,' he said, his voice deepening on a note she had never heard before, but her pulse reacted in response. 'Does that mean anything to you?'

'Just what are you offering me, Simon?' she asked hoarsely, refusing to accept what he was saying.

'Marriage, with all the necessary trimmings, if that's what you want.'

She could no longer avoid the compelling mastery of his gaze, and, despite the fact that her heart did some crazy things inside of her, she was reluctant to grasp at the fragment of hope he was offering while she still so firmly believed that he had every intention of marrying Rosalind. This was not reality; it could only be a cruel desire to inflict further pain.

'Haven't you overlooked something?' she asked, shutting her mind, and her heart, to the inescapable power of those dark eyes as they probed relentlessly beneath the surface of her composure. 'I'm just like Marilyn in your play, remember?'

'You're not like Marilyn at all!' he retorted harshly, close enough to touch her, yet not doing so.

'But you told Godfrey——' she faltered, choking back the tears when she saw comprehension dawning in his eyes.

'I presumed you had been discussing the play, and the remark was never intended to be taken seriously.'

A pulse throbbed wildly in her throat. Was she going mad, or was this true? It would, of course, be just like him to do something like that. Had he not always baited her in every way?

Without intending to, she recalled his remark that evening after the play. 'If there was nothing in the play that was of any significance to you, then I underestimated you completely.'

Suddenly everything was clear, heart-wrenchingly clear as she saw again in her mind the shadowy woman in that final scene, offering escape from bondage.

'Oh, Simon,' she whispered shakily, glimpsing at heaven, but afraid to believe that it was intended for her. 'All I could think of, while Marilyn's character unfolded on the stage, and afterwards, was that this was how you saw me. No wonder you were so angry with me that night when I'd completely missed the subtle message in the finale.' The flames kindling in his eyes told her that she was not mistaken as she asked with added confidence, 'It *was* intended for me, wasn't it?'

His firm mouth softened in a way that made her tremble as he said with a touch of the old mockery, 'Could it have been intended for anyone else, when you're the only one who has the power to set me free?'

She was in his arms then, her tears mingling with her laughter before the pressure of his lips on hers brushed away the final shred of doubt. There was a passionate intensity about his kiss, and in the way he held her, that drew a rapturous response from her. She felt him tremble against her, and knew his need; a need that only she could assuage, but in this moment of extreme happiness there hovered a cloud that might not be so easy to disperse with.

'Simon, what are you going to do about Rosalind?' she asked the moment she was allowed to catch her breath.

His face darkened instantly with an anger that made her thankful that it was not directed at her personally. 'I've already done all there's to be done about her. I told her to pack and leave at once, and, if I'm not mistaken, I heard her car leaving some minutes ago. I don't think she'll come here again.'

His arms tightened about her, but she held him off with her hands against his chest. 'I must know, Simon. Did she have some kind of hold over you?'

'She imagined she had, and I allowed her to continue thinking so,' he explained, his mouth tightening once more. 'She's sponged on me ever since I married her sister, and I saw no reason to discontinue her allowance after Brenda's death ... until now.'

Helen buried her face against his shoulder and heard the heavy beat of his heart as he drew her close to him. She clung to him then, savouring his nearness before she whispered into his neck, 'She made some awful insinuations.'

'That I tried to poison Brenda and finally killed her?'

'Yes.'

'And you didn't believe her?'

'No,' she shook her head against him, recoiling from the idea as she done done so often since hearing those accusations. 'She sounded very convincing, but I just couldn't believe you would kill anyone.'

'Blind trust?'

She looked up at him then and smiled. 'Something like that.'

His eyes darkened with emotion, and she was suddenly crushed painfully against the hard length of his body. 'My God, Helen!' he murmured hoarsely against her throat. 'I've never yet met anyone like you. You're everything that a woman ought to be; gentle, understanding, and with such a great capacity to love.' He raised his head then and looked down at her with a hint of humility and uncertainty that sat oddly upon him. 'You *do* love me, don't you?'

'Haven't I given myself hopelessly away?' she laughed, colouring slightly, but there was no answering smile in his eyes as he drew her towards the sofa.

'Sit down, my dear, there's so much I have to explain

that I'm not quite sure where to begin.'

He did not sit down beside her, and she felt strangely lost without his arms about her as she suggested, 'Why not begin at the very beginning, Simon?'

'The beginning?' he laughed shortly, but there was a familiar edge of bitterness to the sound as he thrust his hands into his pockets and paced the floor characteristically. 'My faith in women was crushed at a youthful age when my mother left my father in her search for wealth. My father died a year later, and that meant the orphanage for me.'

Her instinct to comfort him was very strong, but she suppressed the desire, realising that this was not the moment to interrupt him with a display of sympathy.

'Forgive me, Helen, if some of the things I'm going to say may sound a little crude, but you must know the truth. I knew a fair amount of women before I met Brenda,' he continued after a slight pause, 'but I never took them seriously. Brenda was damned clever, however, at hiding her true character, and, dazzled as I was by her as a person and an actress, I became her lover. It wasn't long before she told me that she was pregnant, and that I would have to marry her. At the time I couldn't quite understand this, because we'd always taken precautions, but I nevertheless accepted it. I married her, and seven months later Peter was born. Our marriage wasn't a success. Brenda loved the stage, and other men just as much. Then she discovered that she was expecting Lisa.' He was silent for a moment, his lip caught between his strong teeth. 'She hurled abuse at me in her fury, and it was then that I discovered the truth.'

Incredible thoughts rushed through Helen's mind as she sat watching him pace about. 'Simon?'

He turned to face her then with a look of such intense bitterness that she almost cried out.

'Peter wasn't my child, Helen,' he confirmed her suspicions, and she knew what an effort it must have been to make this confession.

'And Lisa?' she asked, hating herself.

'Lisa is mine,' he replied firmly, and she felt the tension uncoil within her. 'After learning the truth about Peter, I made sure that the necessary tests were taken. I wanted definite medical proof, and I got it.' His expression hardened. 'After that incident our marriage became a farce. I never told anyone of my discovery, and I never touched her again.'

'Why did Rosalind accuse you of trying to poison Brenda?'

'I think it was basically Rosalind's idea to try and save her sister's tattered reputation, but the truth is that Brenda had been drinking heavily that night and, without realising it, she took a double amount of the capsules the doctor had prescribed for her insomnia.'

'So Rosalind really had no hold over you at all,' Helen remarked with relief.

'None at all,' he smiled briefly. 'I think she eventually believed her own story, for she used it often enough when she needed money, and it amused me to let her think that she was blackmailing me.'

'She led me to believe she'd succeeded in blackmailing you into a marriage with her.'

'The devil she did,' he laughed harshly. 'And you believed her?'

Helen flushed guiltily. 'I didn't know what to believe eventually. She sounded so convincing. But tell me about the accident?' she changed the subject.

'Brenda had insisted that we visit these friends of hers in the country. It was one of those abominable parties, but I needed a break, so I agreed,' he sighed, seating himself on the chair opposite her as if he could not bear to touch her until he had told her everything. 'Half way through the evening, Brenda disappeared, and I soon discovered why when I saw the husband of her friend coming out of one of the bedrooms. I waited a moment and then went in there myself, and I found her beating Lisa, for the obvious reason that the child must have walked in on them. This angered me more than anything else, and, as Brenda had been drinking too much, as usual, I decided it was time we left before there was a scene. Needless to say, we argued until I finally lost my temper and threatened her with violence if she didn't pull herself together. Rosalind heard this, and it was something else she thought she could threaten me with.' His glance held an urgent query. 'Helen . . .'

'I believe you, Simon,' she reassured him quietly. 'Go on.'

'Brenda tried to continue the argument in the car, but I wasn't going to be provoked while I was driving. My silence apparently infuriated her further, and she grabbed the steering wheel in a fit of hysteria. She had the strength of a maniac at that moment, and, because it was so unexpected, the car went out of control and landed half on its nose, half on its side in the ditch.' Pain mingled with bitterness, and it was more than Helen could stand. She bridged the gap between them and sat down on the arm of his chair as she drew his head against her breast. His arms circled her waist instantly, and they held each other close for some time before he drew her down on to his lap. 'Brenda was thrown out of the car by the impact, and crushed under it,' he said in a controlled voice. 'Peter, who had been asleep in an upright position, died instantly, and Lisa . . . Lisa was saved by the mere fact that she was lying down at the time. She was thrown to the floor, and sustained only a few scratches and bruises.'

She placed a gentle hand against his scarred cheek and traced the raised scar with her fingertips as she had longed to do so often. 'And you were left with this.'

'This and crushed ribs,' he said, pressing his lips to the palm of her hand and following it up with a more satisfactory embrace that set her nerves tingling in response.

'Simon, I have to tell you now,' she said eventually, unable to keep this information to herself much longer. 'I discovered the reason for Lisa's nightmares some time ago.'

She related briefly the story Lisa had told her, confirming his suspicion that Lisa had witnessed her mother's indiscretion, and telling him of the promise Lisa had been thrashed into making.

'Dear heaven!' Simon groaned when she had finished. 'No wonder the poor child was almost out of her mind. If only I'd thought to question her, but I believed, as the doctors did, that it was merely as a result of the accident that she was in such a nervous state.'

'It doesn't matter now, and we need never discuss it again, Simon. The past is over now, and there's just the future,' she told him, smoothing away the lines on his forehead, and running her fingers across his cheek to the strong line of his jaw.

'Thanks to you,' he said, his glance softening.

Helen shook her head, dismissing this fact as she glanced at him curiously. 'What were you doing at my aunt's cottage the other night?'

His hands were in her hair, creating sensations she was beginning to know so well. 'I went specifically to ask her if she had any objections to her niece marrying a man like myself.'

Helen understood suddenly the reason for her aunt's odd behaviour that night she had questioned her, and amusement sparkled in her eyes as she looked up at Simon. 'What did she say?'

'After a little friendly persuasion, she gave her approval,' he replied with gentle mockery, then his eyes darkened with emotion. 'I love you, Helen.'

She had waited long to hear him say those words, and now the miracle of it brought tears to her eyes; tears that he brushed away with his lips before he kissed her in a way that sent the blood pulsing through her veins. She clung to him, returning his kisses and caresses with a passion that matched his own.

'When did you know that you loved me?' she asked when he released her slightly and allowed her pulses to settle down to a more regular pace.

He slid a finger across her flushed cheek, and smiled down at her with a warmth that somehow softened his features. 'I think I must have known from the very beginning, that's why I fought so hard against it. I wanted you, but I couldn't trust another woman again.'

'Do you trust me now?'

'With my life.'

'Simon ... I'm not perfect,' she reminded him, a little overawed by his remark.

'Neither am I,' he told her firmly, then, trailing his lips across her cheek and along her throat to where a tell-tale pulse throbbed in response, he asked: 'Will you marry me, my darling?'

My darling! Words she had thought did not belong in his vocabulary, yet they sounded so perfectly right at that moment.

'Yes, I will marry you, darling Simon,' she sighed happily, sliding her hand round to the back of his neck.

'It will have to be soon,' he murmured urgently as he pushed aside the collar of her blouse to explore the smoothness of her shoulder with his lips, and creating delicious havoc with her emotions.

'It will *have* to be soon,' she agreed as desire swept through her and left her trembling wiht the intensity of it.

His sometimes ruthless mouth brushed her lips apart with an expertise that was intended to arouse emotions she had only guessed at before. She felt his shoulder muscles ripple beneath her hands, and then she was lost in a flood of sensations she no longer had the desire to suppress.

'Do you think you could make a real home of Brock Castle?' he asked eventually when she lay flushed and trembling against his chest, listening to the heavy beat of his heart, and thrilling to the knowledge that it was beating just for her.

'Oh, Simon, yes,' she murmured ecstatically. 'Does this mean that you want to stay here permanently, and that Lisa could go to the local school?'

'It does.'

'Darling Simon! This is the most wonderful Christmas present I've ever received,' she told him with a warmth in her eyes that made him draw a sharp breath. 'I love you very, very much,' she added tremulously.

'Say that last bit again,' he commanded, and she did so willingly, offering him her lips.

Lisa chose that moment to burst into the room and she stood regarding them curiously for a moment before she asked, 'Does this mean that you love each other now, and that you're going to be my new mommy, Helen?'

'Yes, darling, it does,' Helen laughed, blushing scarlet as she extricated herself from Simon's arms and slipped off his lap to restore some order to her appearance, carefully avoiding the teasing glint in his eyes.

Lisa gave a whoop of delight, embracing them both with equal fervour. 'Let's go downstairs and have a party. Aunty Ros left ages ago, and that means we can have a really nice party. Just the three of us.'

Helen's glance met Simon's fearfully, but there was laughter in his eyes and a relaxed expression on his usually stern face that made her heart lift with joy at the knowledge that he was free at last.

'We certainly have something to celebrate,' he agreed, placing an arm about each of them. 'I have a bottle of champagne somewhere, and there's lemonade for Lisa, so let's do as she suggests and have a party.'

As they toasted each other some minutes later, Helen

found it difficult to suppress the tears that rose to her eyes. Her happiness was too incredible to believe, and yet it was there in the pressure of his arm about her waist, and in the fire of his eyes as they met hers over the rim of his glass.

There was no longer any need for words, for their eyes were the mirrors of their souls, and soon, very soon, the dream would become a reality, and she would belong to him for ever.

YOUR LOVE-NATURE
EARTH SIGN   July 23 - August 22

Your Leo love-nature is warm, romantic, idealistic and loyal. Leo is the sign that rules the heart; so, not surprisingly, "affairs of the heart" are very important to you. Pride and high self-esteem are among your major characteristics; you are never happy without the admiration and respect of the people around you. But you really glow only when there is one special person whose dependable, devoted love envelops you with warmth.

One of your most charming characteristics is that you idealize the one you love, attributing all sorts of good qualities to him. This tends to bring out the best in your lover, who tries to live up to your high opinion. You will make any sacrifice for love and in fact are romantic enough to welcome obstacles, which you can then overcome to show your devotion. Unfortunately this attitude sometimes leads you astray. A person who needs you appeals to your chivalrous instincts, and thus you tend to become involved, only to find that this person is not worthy of your idealism and loyalty. For this reason Leo is often disappointed in love.

As partners, the other fire signs, Aries and Sagittarius, are very good because they share your idealism and warmth. Another Leo might also suit you, but you both love being noticed and admired, so there would be constant competition for the spotlight. The cooler air signs—Libra, Aquarius and Gemini—enjoy your buoyancy and friendliness, and would probably be content to let you be the "star" as long as they were having fun, too.

And there's still *more* love in

Harlequin Presents...

Do you have a favorite
Harlequin author?
Then here is an
opportunity you must
not miss!